Delia's Way

Olga Berrocal Essex

Arte Público Press
Houston, Texas
1998

This volume is made possible through grants from the National Endowment for the Arts (a federal agency) and the City of Houston through The Cultural Arts Council of Houston, Harris County.

Recovering the past, creating the future

Arte Público Press
University of Houston
Houston, Texas 77204-2090

Cover illustration and design by Giovanni Mora

Berrocal Essex, Olga.
    Delia's Way / by Olga Berrocal Essex.
    p.   cm.
    ISBN 1-55885-232-8 (pbk. : alk. paper)
    I. Title.
PS3552.E742D4   1998
813'.54—dc21   98-12854
                                                             CIP

♾ The paper used in this publication meets the requirements of the American National Standard for Information Sciences—Permanence of Paper for Printed Library Materials, ANSI Z39.48-1984.

8 9 0 1 2 3 4 5 6 7   10 9 8 7 6 5 4 3 2 1

For Jack

Muchas gracias to Linda Feyder, the editor in every writer's dream, and to the members of the Cambria Writers Workshop for invaluable feedback and generosity in encouragement.

In heaven all is contentment,
in hell all is sorrow,
and on earth, which is in between,
we find both.
 —Baltasar Gracián
  Oráculo manual y arte de prudencia
  (The Art of Worldly Wisdom)

Chapter 1

Delia pulled out the stopper of the delicate crystal bottle she held in her hand and brought it close to her nose. The fragrance of her mother's favorite perfume, *Capricho de mujer*, floated up settling where memories begin. *A Woman's Whim* had always been among the presents her father gave her mother on special occasions. Now, years later, Delia summoned the constants of her youth through its soft, flowery scent.

The prismatic bottle of perfume, among others on a silver and glass tray, became a jewel as the early morning sun filtered through a nearby window. A light breeze caressed the white lace curtains and lifted a corner of the lace runner that protected the polished mahogany dresser top like a veil over the shoulders of a sun kissed bride.

Delia picked up the tube of mascara. Looking in the mirror, she applied the wand to her eyelashes and noticed tiny lines around her dark brown eyes. She opened them wide and blinked to erase the lines.

The oval mirror, framed in mahogany, also gave her a glimpse of a fading scar on the back of her hand. She hadn't noticed the scar for a long time. Now it seemed to want her attention. Its smooth center just missed being completely round because of the short marks around the edge, like the rays of the sun that had nearly obliterated the scar with a deep tan.

When she finished applying her makeup, she pumped hand lotion from a container and began to massage her hands, her left thumb slowly caressing the scar.

Delia closed her eyes.

The mixture of sugar and water gurgled, boiling in the small aluminum pan over the flame of the gas stove burner. Nine-year-old Delia stood on a wooden crate leaning forward, watching the sweet

1

concoction her sister María Elena stirred with a wooden spoon. Once in a while, María Elena let a drop or two fall in a bowl of cool water to see if the caramel hardened instantly. Then she would pour the mixture into small paper cones set on a rack to cool.

Delia's mouth had begun to water. The sweet smell of caramel wafting with the heat waves almost made her swoon.

"This is the second batch today. How many are you making, María Elena?" Delia reached for a spoon to dip in the boiling caramel and maybe get a taste. Her hand moved over the pot and a drop of boiling caramel fell, branding her as it sizzled.

"Aaeee! No! Aaeeee!"

The parakeet flew from his perch and landed on the back of a dining chair, screeching, shedding some loose green feathers, and matching Delia's cry when she dropped the spoon on the floor and held her hand.

Her eyes filled with tears and her heartbeat raced at the speed of fear as she looked at María Elena, who smiled, still holding the wooden spoon poised to drop more hot caramel on Delia's hand.

Crying, Delia plunged her hand in the bowl of water.

"I'll tell Mamá, I swear!" Rage ripped the words from her throat, but it didn't stop her tears nor the pain.

María Elena turned her back, walked to a drawer and pulled out a butcher knife. She suddenly turned toward Delia and held the knife's sharp point to her own stomach. Coming within a breath from Delia's face, María Elena bit off her words one by one, driving their meaning into Delia's brain.

"You know what will happen then, don't you? I'll kill myself! I'll do it with this knife. I'll plunge it deep inside me, like this!"

María Elena moved the knife to one side, then the other, without penetrating the fabric of her loose cotton dress.

Tears continued to flow from Delia's eyes and her throat tightened under the grip of an invisible fist. She held her breath, stared at her sister, then at her blistered hand. When Delia looked up again, María Elena raised her head, tightened her lips, faked the slashing of her own belly once more.

Delia saw green flashes behind María Elena's narrowed eyelids and screamed.

"No! Nena! No more!"

Satisfied that her trick had worked once again, María Elena dropped the knife on the counter and tossed back her long braid. She quickly grabbed a potholder, lifted the hot pan and turned off the burner. The acrid smell of burned caramel permeated the kitchen.

"You see what you made me do? Now the pan is burned. There'll be no more caramel today!"

María Elena barked so close to Delia's face that her spit mixed with her sister's tears. María Elena dropped the pan in the sink, grabbed one of Delia's pigtails and pulled her toward the refrigerator.

The parakeet screeched again, echoing Delia's scream.

"Come here and shut up!" María Elena said. "Let me put some butter on your hand. And when Mamá comes home from the store, you better remember: It was all your fault for getting in the way."

Delia wiped her face with a dishtowel and ran up the stairs to the room she shared with her sister. She threw herself on her bed and sobbed.

Outside, rain began to pour. She heard it play a *tamborito* on the rusted corrugated roof of the potting shed. It would wash the mangos weighing down the branches of the old tree that shaded the patio. She looked out the window at the tops of coconut palm trees leaning in the wind, their fronds sparkling in the tropical sunlight filtering through the clouds. She started to close the shutters next to María Elena's bed, but she looked at the blister beginning to raise on her hand and changed her mind. She leaned out the window and let the warm rain wash away her tears.

Back in her bed, she lay down again on her side, folding up her legs, feeling a giant fist squeezing all the space from her throat to her belly. She watched raindrops slowly soak a corner of María Elena's bedspread. She didn't want to cry anymore and closed her eyes, squeezing her eyelids hard to keep the tears inside.

"My mother. The mother of my mother. The mother of the mother of my mother. The mother of the mother of the mother of my mother . . ."

Delia repeated her own childish mantra, going back, back in time, erasing all other thoughts, stacking her feelings up carefully, one on top of the other like the grains of dirt she had watched the ants push up from holes on the ground in her mother's garden, forming mounds that betrayed their presence underground. Deep sighs and short sobs punctuated the restless sleep that followed.

Delia woke up startled when her mother's lips touched her swollen eyelids. The side of her face felt wet from lying on the pillowcase drenched with her tears. She closed her eyes when her mother's soft hands caressed her forehead and smoothed her hair, lifting away the few strands that had stuck to her forehead and her cheeks.

"María Elena told me what happened, darling. I am so sorry you had an accident. Your hand must hurt so much. Let me see . . ." Mamá lifted Delia's hand, examined the blistered burn and winced.

"You need to be careful with this, *hija*, keep it dry. We'll burst it and dress it tonight before you go to sleep. Now it's time to get ready for supper. Your Papá will be home soon and Juliana is setting the table."

Mamá's kiss was cool on Delia's forehead and the bedsprings sighed a little when she stood up.

She watched her mother walk out of the room, leaving behind the faint scent of her perfume. She barely knew this woman, who spoke to her friends in whispers. Who, with just a look, signaled Delia to obey, to become invisible and speechless; to refrain from searching out the secrets that seemed to inhabit their home where Juliana polished the furniture daily, waxed the tiled floors once a week, and saved eggshells to feed the flowers in the garden. Juliana also walked down Salsipuedes street with Mamá to the noisy, smelly central market by the bay every morning. They carried canvas bags to bring back the fresh food that was served at the table for breakfast, and later for lunch and dinner as soon as Papá walked in from work at the printing shop.

Along with the bags of food, *Doña* Berta Pineda and Juliana brought back from the market the latest gossip being broadcast and expanded until it reached the farther limits of the fertile imagination of the *doñas* and their *criadas*.

Delia got up, rushed to the bathroom, shut the door and pulled down her panties. She almost didn't make it.

"How can I pee so much, when I already cried so much?" To her, that made as little sense as cousin Justo's presence in their midst.

Justo Salazar had appeared at the Pineda's doorstep four days before, carrying a change of clothes in a paper bag and cradling a ripe pineapple on one arm like a mother carries a nursing baby.

Mamá had welcomed the lean, balding man as if she had been expecting him. She had smiled and set aside her crochet work when Juliana ushered him in.

Justo handed the pineapple to Juliana and let the paper bag drop to the floor. Then he embraced Mamá.

"Oh, Justo, Justo, I am so glad to see you! You are here at last!" Mamá whispered, her voice breaking. She wiped tears from her eyes and showed him to a rocker in the *sala,* then sat on the sofa across from him.

"Juliana, bring some coffee, please," she called out, without taking her eyes off him.

Soon after, Justo sipped hot black coffee, rocking across from Mamá, who beamed as she poured a cup for herself.

When Justo took a second sip of coffee and his eyes surveyed the room, he met Delia's. She sat on the floor near the window, a few jacks spread in front of her. Her hand was poised in mid air, holding a small red ball.

The first detail Delia noticed about the man was the light blue color of his eyes, as clear as a mountain pool. Blue eyes were as uncommon in her family as the fact that, so far, he hadn't said anything about where he was coming from, not even to remark on what kind of weather he had left behind.

When Mamá saw them looking at each other, she snapped her fingers and gave Delia "the look."

Delia bit her lips and gathered the jacks. She looked back once, before she walked out the door and saw his blue eyes again over the rim of the cup. Outside, she turned again. Mamá was at the window, her head tilted, and Delia knew she would have to stay away.

That evening, Justo ate supper at the table with the rest of the family.

"This is my cousin Justo and he will be staying with us for a while," Mamá had said to María Elena and Delia when they first sat down to dinner. She didn't offer any other explanation and neither did Papá.

Delia grew more curious when, during the meal, the grownups' conversation revealed nothing about Justo. She glanced at him at every opportunity. When she caught his eye, he smiled at her, a gold tooth glinting under the light of the lamp that hung from the ceiling.

Delia made a mental note: *campesino*. Only people who came from the interior flashed gold-filled smiles, while *capitalinos* in the city shunned the custom as barbaric.

While Delia and María Elena helped Juliana gather the dishes from the table, Papá, Mamá and Justo went into the *sala* to take their coffee and, apparently, to plan Justo's future because the next day Justo went to work for Papá at the printing shop. Juliana had set up a cot for him in the small room next to hers. It was the room used mostly for sorting and ironing laundry and storing odds and ends.

Delia had let three days pass, waiting for more signals that would flag Justo's history. Finally, last night after supper, when Papá was resting in the hammock at the back porch blowing smoke rings to amuse her, Delia had ventured her own inquiry.

"Papá, why is Justo staying here with us?"

"Because he has nowhere else to go, *querida*."

"What about his family? Doesn't he have a wife?"

"We are his family, Delia. He is your Mamá's cousin. The rest of his family is in Aguadulce. Just a few cousins." Papá blew another smoke ring. "He had a wife. Once."

"What happened to her?"

"Ah, *querida*, you are too young to know."

That again! "Too young" was getting tiresome.

Delia rushed in, "I am not too young to see Joe Louis fight. We are still going to see the fight, aren't we?"

"You bet! Once in a lifetime. Joe Louis in Panamá. Not a championship fight, but a fight with the best boxer in the world. Right here. We won't miss it."

"So then. Tell me about Justo, Papá. He's staying here, I want to know."

Papá blew another smoke ring, taking his time.

"You have to promise, Delia, you won't repeat what I tell you. To anyone. ¿*Sí*? Especially to your Mamá. It's just between you and me." He bridged the space between them with his index finger. "And after I tell you, you'll forget it right off," Papá gestured as if erasing words in the air and the cigarette tip drew a zig-zag of light. "Not to mention it again?"

"*Sí, sí*, Papá. I promise!" Delia placed her open hand over her chest, right where she imagined her heart to be.

Papá hesitated. He measured her commitment with a long, slow look.

"Justo's wife is dead."

Papá waited. That was not enough for Delia. She still sat on the concrete porch step near the hammock, her chin on her knees, waiting while Papá took another drag from his cigarette. She had promised. He better deliver.

"A crime of passion," Papá said, his voice so low she almost didn't hear him.

Two perfect smoke rings floated over Papá. He coughed and flipped what was left of the cigarette. Delia followed its arc until it landed on the dirt, next to a lemon tree.

It was very dark now. The cicadas began their nightly serenade and the night-blooming jasmine that climbed the post where Delia leaned, scented the night. Beyond the garden wall, the neighbor's dog yapped.

"So? What's that?" she asked.

"What?"

"A crime of passion," Delia said, leaning forward.

Papá sighed. He always did when she pressed him for answers. He sat up in the hammock and pushed slightly with his bare feet to start a slow swinging motion. He looked up at the crescent moon.

"They had been married just three years and one day Justo found his wife with another man. He went to the shed where they kept the machetes he used to cut the sugar cane. When he came back, the man had left. But she was still there. He cut her throat with the machete."

Papá looked at Delia.

She gasped and her mouth remained open. Her heart was beating so hard, she put her hands over her chest as if to stop it. That didn't help. She pressed her chest once more, her fingers together, to keep her racing heart from escaping. Her gaze remained fixed on Papá's face until she found her voice in a whisper.

"He killed her?" Delia swallowed bitter saliva.

"Yes, *querida*. He was tried and sentenced. He has paid for his debt to society. He has just finished serving ten years in Coiba."

"Coiba . . ." Delia whispered. She stood up and sat in the hammock next to Papá.

The night was sultry, but Delia suddenly felt cold. She needed to feel human warmth. She needed her father's arms around her.

He complied.

Delia's mind raced. Coiba. The penal colony for hardened criminals in an island off the Gulf, from which there was no escape. Some never came back alive.

Papá held Delia close to him. She could smell the scent of cigarette smoke on his white undershirt, the lingering spice of his aftershave, just under his chin.

"But he is free now, Papá?"

"*Sí, hija*. The jury said it was a crime of passion. He loved her very much and jealousy made him kill her. That is why he only served ten years."

"But she is dead! Dead forever!" Delia said softly, trying to comprehend the vagaries of man-made justice.

"Crimes of passion can be understood, *querida*. It's a matter of betrayal by a loved one. It's a matter of a man's honor," Papá said, as if, measured with that rule, the crime became less violent, less severe.

"A man's honor," Delia said to her image in the bathroom mirror above the white tiled sink and finished washing her face in cool water, using only her left hand to keep the burn dry. She felt the sting of the burn on her hand and on her soul and held back tears.

Walking down the stairs, Delia looked at the blister.

A crime of passion. With a machete. A crime of passion. With a knife? The two images bounced in her mind and she winced, like she had done in the brief time since Justo had entered her life and she had become aware of his shadowy past.

Justo didn't show up at dinner time.

"Is Justo working late tonight?" Mamá asked, lifting the lid off the soup toureen.

"He is looking for a place to rent, Berta, he needs to be on his own. I advanced him three weeks pay," Papá explained. He winked at Delia.

Before Delia went to bed for the night, her mother pierced the blister on her hand, dressed the burn with Vaseline, and bandaged it. Delia couldn't see the blister now, but the pain remained to remind her. She didn't speak to María Elena that evening. In her dreams, Juliana placed the neck of a live chicken on a wooden block and whacked its head off with a machete.

Chapter 2

Two days later, the burn on Delia's hand had stopped oozing and Justo announced that he had rented a room in a tenement building. After he moved out of the Pineda home, Delia still saw him often, because she spent a great deal of time at Papá's printing shop, watching him work and running errands for him.

Each time Delia entered the shop, the smell of printing ink welcomed her, just as incense embraced her when she entered the church. The roar, clang, and roll of the printing machines delighted her. She watched the freshly printed pages fall like sheets blown from a clothesline, one on top of the other, completing the first step on their journey to feed a hungry mind.

Conversation at the printing shop was kept to a minimum dictated by the noise of the printing presses. This gave Delia ample opportunity to observe. She looked at Justo, searching for a gesture, some fierce distinguishing quality that would tag a murderer. But she found none. When she stared too much, Papá would walk by and give her shoulder a reassuring squeeze.

Justo counted out glossy pages from large reams of the finest quality paper and stacked them on the printing presses. Delia watched him pour viscous inks for the rollers, carefully spreading the ink evenly with a large spatula to avoid blotches when the words and images were imprinted on the paper. He also mixed just the right amount of glue beads with water and boiled the mixture to the proper consistency for the sticky mucilage that joined together stitched sections of books. After the books were assembled, Justo trimmed the pages so their even edges would accept the gilding finish Papá applied to special tomes.

After Papá pulled on surgical rubber gloves, he brushed a thin coat of sizing on the book edges and waited until it was tacky. Papá chewed the corner of his lower lip in deep concentration. Delia held her breath when her father picked up the strips of gold leaf with a soft brush and placed them over the sizing. This was done with precision. Papá didn't compromise on the quality of the fine books he produced for his clients, including the Jesuits who ran private schools in the city and served the parish where the printing shop was located.

Delia admired Justo's dedication to work. His glances at the good-looking women that passed by the shop's window or walked in to transact business amused her. It amazed her that Justo could detect a pair of high heels clicking on the sidewalk, over the noise of the printing presses. Young women seemed eager to speak with him, overlooking his incipient baldness and drinking in the calm blueness of his eyes and the flashy smile that deepened the creases on his cheeks where dimples once had cutely touched the face of a carefree boy.

Was this awareness of the other sex what led to crimes of passion? This was one of the many questions bouncing in Delia's mind like ping pong balls. An endless game going on too long for her own liking.

Three months after Justo moved out, Delia, Juliana, Mamá, and María Elena busied themselves in the shady *sala*, where the electric ceiling fan kept the late afternoon air moving and pulled in the fragrance of orange blossoms. Delia sat on the floor, bent over a sewing sampler, while María Elena grew impatient with the dial of the short-wave radio.

"XEW is not coming in," she whined to Mamá, the shrill static squeals backing her up.

The radio station from Mexico City brought them their favorite *boleros* when it was clear of static. Today, radio reception proved impossible. So María Elena settled for a local station and the loud, rapid-fire delivery of the announcer inviting all listeners to a fire sale at the five and dime that had burned down the week before. The *danzón* that followed the commercial reprieved them.

María Elena moved her head to the rhythm of the music. She stood up, raised both arms and faced the draft of the electric fan. She leaned over Delia and watched her stitch a buttonhole in the sewing sampler.

"Her stitches are not close enough, Mamá. Some are shorter than others. And that white thread is turning black from her dirty hands!" María Elena grabbed the sampler from Delia's hands and shoved it at *Doña* Berta.

Delia saw the two strands of thread slip through the eye of the needle she held between her fingers.

Mamá took the sampler, examined the buttonhole, and gave it back to Delia.

"She just needs to practice," Mamá said. "It will get better."

María Elena dropped her shoulders, showing her disappointment that Mamá had not taken a tougher stand.

"Would you pick us some lemons for lemonade, Nena?" Mamá called out, as María Elena walked out, slamming the door to the patio.

"Why is she always doing that, Mamá? She hates me!" Delia said shifting on the floor, crossing her legs, squinting when she tried to thread the needle looking through the moisture welling in her eyes.

"She just wants you to do things right, *hija*. Like she does. Nena doesn't hate you. She only wants you to learn."

Delia bit her lip and a salty drop dampened the buttonhole. On the radio, a guitar, violin, and *tambor* combo backed the squeaky voice of a folk singer wailing a *mejorana*.

Juliana, shelling peas, cleared her throat and leaned toward Mamá.

"Isabel told me that she is moving in with Justo soon," Juliana said. "It seems she ate watermelon and swallowed the seeds."

Delia bent forward from the waist and tried to tune out the music from the radio.

Mamá stabbed at her needlepoint, looked out beyond the window to where María Elena picked lemons and gathered them in her skirt. She turned back to Juliana.

"I saw that coming," Mamá said. "It was just a matter of whose watermelon seed sprouted first. Aminta was also seen with him. They know about him, his past, but I guess they just can't stay away from that flashing gold tooth and God knows what else. When women reach marrying age, they look to fish from whatever stream is available." Mamá took another stitch. "Justo's a good man. He'll take care of Isabel."

Delia continued sewing, as if she had not heard the whispers that had started a buzz in her head, like an errant bee.

She knew Isabel was Ana's daughter and that, too, was hard to explain. Ana, a mulatto woman who took in laundry, had no husband and had raised three children. Tito was a school teacher and Beto was studying to be an engineer. Delia had heard Juliana remark to Papá that Tito was *mujeriego*, a woman chaser and that, to make up for it, Beto had turned out *maricón*.

Isabel was Ana's jewel and the odd one in the family. Unlike her mother and brothers, Isabel had a very light complexion, green eyes, and a long, thick, shiny black mane. After each shampoo, Isabel sat outside on her balcony and combed her hair, letting the sun caress the black silk that Papá called Isabel's crowning glory and a road to a man's perdition. Delia looked at it differently. To her, Isabel's hair was a *mantilla* that sometimes was adorned with the embroidery of a red carnation.

Juliana finished shelling the peas. She laid aside the basket, picked up the hem of her dress and began fanning her legs. Delia caught this with the corner of her eye and took it as a sign that Juliana was ready to gossip some more.

Delia stretched her legs, scratched an ankle and moved closer to the women.

"Isabel is working at a pharmacy now," Juliana whispered to Mama. "She stocks shelves, takes in prescriptions and minds the cash register. I guess Ana likes that, because she can get her stinky asafetida for nearly nothing."

Delia heard Mamá giggle. "She had the patches on today. She had a headache again. The odor of fresh asafetida trailed behind her at the market this morning." Mamá's remark sounded more teasing than conspiratorial.

Delia heard the clicking of Mamá's scissors snipping off the end of a strand of yarn on the back of her needlepoint and watched Juliana cross herself and look heavenward.

"Those so-called headaches! Her neighbor told me that Ana gets those pounding headaches the days after she goes gathering. Haven't

13

you heard, *Doña* Berta? The rumor is that on moonless nights Ana sheds her body sack, turns into a goat, and roams the alleys and gardens gathering herbs and filth for her potions. She is a *bruja*!" Juliana crossed herself again, but that act of piety didn't restrain her. "How else could you explain her giving birth to Isabel. So unlike her mother and her brothers. And no one ever saw a man around Ana . . ."

Delia kept her head bent over her sampler, but she turned it from one woman to the other, the corners of her eyes catching the action.

"Oh, Juliana, people will make things up when they don't know everything," Mamá said, and her voice sounded almost angry. "Those are just malicious stories. You don't really believe any of that, do you? Ana's sin is that she keeps to herself and her work and her kids. Some people can't understand that. Do you think Isabel would be in the pickle she seems to be in if Ana knew anything about *brujería*?" Mamá cut a long piece of blue yarn in half and threaded the needle.

"Maybe, *Doña* Berta, but I doubt her kids were conceived from the Espíritu Santo!" Juliana sounded a bit defensive.

Disappointed when Mamá refused to take the bait, Juliana picked up her basket of shelled peas. The slapping sound of her old leather slippers on the tile floor faded away as Juliana made her way to the kitchen.

Why would swallowing watermelon seeds make Isabel move in with Justo? After all, Delia had swallowed a few seeds herself without ill results.

Months later, Isabel showed up at the printing shop wearing a maternity smock and complaining of severe back pain. Justo helped her to a bench next to a stack of printing ink cans and she waited while he went into the back room.

Isabel started to fan herself with her hand.

"Could I get you some water?"

"That would be nice, Delia. Thanks."

Isabel took in a deep breath and placed both hands under the enormous bulge of her belly. She straightened her back, raised her head and moaned softly.

Delia poured cool water into a cup from a bottle that Papá kept in a small refrigerator behind his desk and hurried to Isabel's side.

Isabel took the cup and, after a few sips, she began to moan again about the time Justo returned buttoning the cuffs of his blue chambray shirt.

"*Ya nos vamos, mi amor,*" Justo said to Isabel, helping her off the bench. He turned his worried eyes to Delia. "Please, *chiquilla*, stay here until your Papá returns and tell him I'll be back as soon as I can."

Delia nodded and watched them walk out and hail a cab.

Delia leaned on the door frame, stuffed her hands in her skirt pockets and bit her lower lip. She had not seen Isabel in many months and now she knew why. She was expecting a baby. And judging by Justo's apparent lack of interest in other women since Juliana announced that Isabel was moving in with him, he must be the father. Since there had been no wedding, Mamá would say these two were "living in sin." If Isabel had a father, he would throw her out of his life, she would be dead to him. At least that is what she had overheard Papá say he would do if any of his daughters allowed a man to deceive them, "*si se dejan burlar de un hombre,*" Papá had said.

The dinner hour had passed. Delia played dominoes with María Elena out on the porch when Mamá came out to tell Papá that Isabel had given birth to a baby boy.

"I told Justo to be sure and get that child baptized right away before he starts wearing asafetida patches behind his ears!" Mamá said.

Papá had taken a puff from his cigarette. He laughed so hard that he started coughing. Mamá walked by the hammock on her way to the kitchen to fetch a drink for him and Papá reached over and slapped her buttocks.

Delia laughed too. She knew what they were teasing about and she was winning at dominoes. María Elena wasn't paying attention. She had been studying hard for the admission test she would take the next day at the private high school she planned to attend and her mind seemed far from the game.

Chapter 3

Delia heard the squeal of a car's brakes and looked out the printing shop's window. She saw Brother Cristóbal step out of his station wagon and kick its door shut.

His chin set, frowning and leaning forward, the Jesuit entered Papá's printing shop like a cyclone, ruffling the top pages on a stack of paper Justo had stored on a shelf moments before. Brother Cristóbal only glanced at Papá on his way to Justo, who was inking the rollers on the monstrous offset printer.

Brother Cristóbal's hands fell like clamps on Justo's shoulders. "Stop that! We have to talk!"

Startled, Justo turned around so quickly he almost dumped a tub of yellow ink down the front of Brother Cristóbal's black soutane. He put down the tub and the spatula on the stained and scored top of a wooden table. He wiped his hands on a rag that had started white but had now matured into a rainbow of ink stains that resembled a Kandinsky composition and smelled of thinner fluid.

"What is it, *padre*, can't it wait?"

Brother Cristóbal brushed his tonsure with a swift, impatient hand and raised his voice.

"Why should it? You certainly didn't wait for the good Lord's blessing before you got busy increasing the population of heretics in this town!"

Papá winked at Delia when she looked at him and silently, with a tilt of his head, motioned her to come to him. Fishing some coins from the pocket on his canvas apron, he escorted Delia to the door.

"Go and see if you can find us some *pastelitos* at the bakery, *querida*."

Delia knew the errand was a ploy to get her away from action that promised to be exciting if not explosive.

When she returned to the shop, she found Papá alone.

"Where are Brother Cristóbal and Justo, Papá? I brought enough *pastelitos* for them," she said, surveying the shop.

"They left, *querida*. Let's see what you have here."

16

Papá pushed aside a stack of papers and envelopes to clear space on his desk for both of them. He took the treats out of the brown paper bag that Delia handed him.

She closed in on him, inclining her head, her eyebrows arched.

"It's Justo's business, Delia. Not ours."

That ended it. She sat on the stool opposite Papá, sighed and bit hard on a savory pastry.

Justo's son, Toñito, was three weeks old and crying in Ana's arms, when Isabel became *Señora* de Salazar at the intimate sunset wedding ceremony that preceded his baptism. Brother Cristóbal officiated over both events at the holy altar of the Church of San José, pleased to bring three new souls to the presence of the Lord.

Justo's black suit, white shirt and yellow bow tie were new. His black shoes were not, but they had been professionally shined by the shoeshine boy who lived downstairs from the small apartment Justo shared with Isabel and Toñito. Justo's light brown hair had been carefully trimmed and fluffed, his bald spot artfully disguised.

When he saw Isabel walk up to him in the church on the arm of her brother Tito, Justo smiled and his gold tooth mirrored the light of the candles burning at the altar.

Isabel wore a brocade suit, white nylon stockings and ivory brocade pumps. Something new. A small crown of orange blossoms rested on her black hair that hung down to her waist, whisps of it moving like delicate wings as she walked. She carried in her hands a single yellow rose tied with a long, trailing blue silk ribbon. Something blue. She wore her grandmother's tiny pearl stud earrings and the single strand pearl choker she borrowed from *Doña* Berta. Something old, something borrowed.

Ivory brocade. Motherhood had robbed Isabel of the virginal white dress with a train and veil. That was tradition, too. The rose in her hand trembled perceptibly throughout the brief ceremony.

Justo and Isabel had tears in their eyes when they promised each other love "until death."

Somehow, Delia knew that if death separated these two, it would not be by Justo's hand. She didn't know much about love between a man and a woman, but she sensed that Isabel would never betray Justo Salazar and that Justo would love Isabel de Salazar forever.

María Elena and Juliana served rum punch at the reception hosted by *Don* Ignacio Pineda and his wife *Doña* Berta, at their home.

Isabel's brothers were there too, glad to see Isabel married and grateful to *Don* Nacho for pressing the issue with Brother Cristóbal. Now they would no longer have to endure the gossip about their sister being Justo's *mujer*.

"Thank you, *Don* Nacho. I know you talked to Brother Cristóbal about Toñito. Justo and Isabel are impulsive and didn't wait for God's blessing. But all has been made right now," Ana had said to Papá after he offered a toast to the happiness of the newly-weds.

"My pleasure, Ana, my great pleasure," Papá said, putting an arm round her shoulder. "Justo and Berta are cousins. My Berta always had a special place in her heart for him. He is a good man who met with some bad luck a long time ago. The man hasn't changed, but his luck has and that makes all the difference."

Papá and Ana raised their goblets of rum punch once more.

It disappointed Delia that Ana was not wearing asafetida patch-es behind her ears. Instead, she caught a whiff of *Evening in Paris* when Ana walked by. Mamá had made Ana's shantung dress for the wedding. They had chosen a color they called "ashes of roses" because, Mamá had said, it flattered Ana's dark olive skin and brown eyes. Ana's legs, usually bare, were fashionably covered in white silk stockings. Simple white leather pumps completed her special look for her daughter's wedding.

Somehow the veil of mystery which Delia imagined surround-ed Ana was peeling away to reveal a common, but reserved, woman who didn't seem too concerned with what others thought of her or her family. When Delia saw Ana with her grandson, the arms that held Toñito with such devotion were not the arms of a *bruja*.

As for Ana's oldest son, Tito, he lived up to his fame as a wom-anizer. He had come to the wedding in his best white sharkskin suit, which was too hot for the tropics but was the latest imported fashion. He finished the outfit with brown wingtips. His wide tie had a palm tree and a Hawaiian dancer printed on it. Tito's straight black hair, slicked with pomade, glistened.

Once in a while Tito whipped out from his pants' back pocket a monogrammed handkerchief and patted his face where drops of perspiration moistened his olive skin and threatened to sting his eyes behind horn-rims. He dabbed gently at his black pencil-thin mustache and placed the same handkerchief between his hand and the hand of his dance partner of the moment.

Jealous husbands gave Tito dirty looks when he danced with their wives, held them close and whispered to them, but none of them dared start a fight at the Pineda's house. Mamá and Papá would not have tolerated such a breach of decorum.

Isabel's younger brother, Beto, was more subdued. He wore a pale blue *camisilla*, open at the neck, navy trousers and polished black loafers. He held hands with Justo's former girlfriend Aminta most of the evening.

Delia dismissed the rumors of Beto's effeminacy. His manner toward Aminta was less aggressive than Tito's behavior toward his dance partners. Still, Delia didn't see in Beto the hand-flapping and swishing she had observed in the *maricones* that dressed as women at Carnaval time.

Chalk one up for Mamá. She had been right sometime back when Juliana first announced that Isabel was moving in with Justo, and Mamá had said that Juliana shouldn't pay attention to gossip about Ana and her family. Delia saw nothing sinister enough to label Ana a *bruja* and her sons were nothing out of the ordinary.

The young man in charge of the music began to play a *pasillo* and, with a look and a smile, Papá invited Mamá to dance. She followed him to the *sala*, where the newlyweds and other couples already moved to the romantic rhythm of the music.

Delia went outside to look at them through the open window, framing them for the album of her memories.

Papá looked so handsome in the crisp, custom-made white *camisilla* that accentuated his deeply tanned skin. Shiny black leather shoes mirrored the hem of his black drill trousers. When he

19

danced with Mamá, he held her like a porcelain figurine, the thumb of his right hand slightly touching the middle of her back, the fingers gracefully extended. With his other hand, he made a gentle cradle where Mamá rested her manicured hand where an emerald caught the light, competing with the diamond ring on the hand that rested lightly on Papá's shoulder.

Mamá wore a calf-length, light blue taffeta dress with matching pumps for the occasion and had her dark brown hair caught on a French twist held by gold combs adorned with pearls. Last Christmas Papá had given Mamá the pearl drop earrings she wore to Isabel's wedding.

Delia rested her elbow on the window sill and her face on the palm of her hand. Smiling, she brushed back hair that the soft breeze kept blowing over her face. She longed for the day when she would dance as Mamá did. When she would be held in the arms of a handsome husband who would summon her by pursing his lips and whistling his unique call, just as Papá whistled when Mamá, María Elena, or Delia were beyond the range of his voice.

Near midnight, the last guest left the reception and Mamá kicked off her shoes near the kitchen door. She dipped some punch and filled two goblets. She gave one to Juliana, who stacked dishes in the sink with Delia's help.

"You must be tired, Juliana, just leave those now and start the cleaning early in the morning. They all loved the wedding cake. I can't thank you enough."

Delia watched them touch glasses together in mutual congratulations. She knew they were happy for the success of the party, for Justo, Isabel, and Toñito. She had seen an understanding surface between the two women during the preparations for the wedding, an eagerness on Mamá's part to obliterate Isabel's shame, to make things right for Justo, with the servant acquiescent to those wishes.

Juliana untied her apron, hung it from a hook behind the kitchen door and went to her own room in the back of the house.

Delia cut a small piece of leftover *sopa borracha*, the rum-saturated cake that Juliana had made for the wedding.

"It's good night for you too, *hija*. Had a good time?" Mamá stroked Delia's head.

"*Sí*, Mamá. I like weddings, even with all the crying that goes on."

"Then I promise not to cry at yours," Mamá teased.

"May I have this last piece of *sopa borracha* before I go to bed, Mamá?"

Doña Berta kissed Delia's cheek and whispered in hear ear, "And that's all. You've had too much already and I know who will wake up tomorrow with a hangover!"

Delia sat down to eat the cake and Mamá walked out to join Papá and María Elena, who were accompanying Brother Cristóbal to the entry gate.

"That *hijo de puta!*"

Delia froze. The piece of cake fell off the fork half way to her mouth.

Papá's voice crashed the murmurs of the late night. He was swearing and he was swearing big. He wasn't the type of man who would call someone a son-of-a-bitch and he was doing it in front of Brother Cristóbal.

The Jesuit sounded conciliatory. "I will talk to Pablo, Nacho. I will try to convince him that he has to give in. The nuns are adamant. They won't admit María Elena unless she is recognized."

María Elena sobbed, "Oh, Mamá, Mamá!" while Mamá tried to shush her.

Papá's leather heels tapped his impatience on the patio tiles. "She will be thirteen when the school term starts, Brother. All these years I have been wanting to adopt her legally and that *cabrón* has been in the way."

Delia heard her mother trying to quiet down Papá. "Keep your voice down, Nacho, the neighbors . . ."

Papá ignored Mamá's plea and Delia imagined him shaking off Mamá's calming touch when she heard him say, "*¡Al carajo con los vecinos!*"

The crude epithet burned in her ears and Delia winced. Papá's temperament didn't mix well with liquor.

"By every measure that counts she is a Pineda, Brother Cristóbal," Papá was saying and his voice softened. "You know I love her as I do my own daughter. I am raising her as my own *hija*. When I married her mother I took María Elena into my heart too." His voice became angry again. "And she will have the best education I can get her even if I have to tear off that *cabrón*'s *cojones!*"

Delia thought that perhaps she should flee the kitchen, get away from the scene to which she was an unwilling, unnoticed witness. She thought about Papá. He had been celebrating. He had danced with Mamá. He had drunk a lot of rum punch and beer. Now someone crossed him and all was boiling over. It had to do with María Elena, the nuns, someone named Pablo and, despite herself, there was no way Delia was going to leave the kitchen where the open window allowed her to hear Papá and the others. She wished she could see them, but that might reveal her own presence. She sensed that this outburst from Papá had some meaning in her own life.

She set the fork on the plate quietly and listened.

This time Mamá pleaded with Brother Cristóbal. "Nena already passed the school admission test, Brother. Do the nuns have to see that birth certificate before they say yes?"

"Those are the rules, *Doña* Berta. The students at La Santísima Concepción are all legitimate in the eyes of God and of men. In the public school she could pass for a Pineda. But this is different. The nuns don't want to deal with scandal," Brother Cristóbal said.

Papá stopped pacing. "This will be resolved before the end of the week, Brother, or my name isn't Ignacio Pineda! You may speak to Pablo about it if you wish. But I will find him tomorrow even if I have to sit in court and wait until he finishes arguing a case. I have waited more than ten years for him to agree to this."

There was a brief pause, when the only sound coming from outside was María Elena's sniffling.

"Berta, *mi amor*, take María Elena inside. I'll walk Brother Cristóbal to his car," Papá said.

Mamá's voice broke, "Good night, Brother Cristóbal, and thank you for everything."

When Mamá opened the door and walked up the stairs with María Elena, Delia heard her sister still sobbing.

"*Ya, ya, hija,*" Mamá whispered. "Stop crying, Nena, Nacho will take care of it . . ." The sound of her voice faded as mother and daughter climbed the stairs.

Delia frowned. It was odd that Mamá had referred to Papá as "Nacho" when she spoke to María Elena, as if he were a stranger, not her father.

"She's not his real daughter. She's not my sister!" Delia whispered so low, afraid to hear her own voice confirming the devastating truth that had ended what had been a day of joy and now squeezed her heart into a cruel fist.

With trembling hands she scooped the piece of cake from the table onto the saucer. She took her time cleaning up the mess. Her temples throbbed with the pounding of her pulse, but she was in no rush to go upstairs and face María Elena in their room. She didn't want to face Papá either, so she went in the *sala,* turned off the lights, and lay down on the sofa, trying to warm herself under Mama's crocheted afghan.

"My mother. The mother of my mother . . ."

Delia's litany stopped. It was replaced by the memory of her grandmother's funeral when she was seven years old.

She remembered the suffocating heat in the crowded funeral parlor and Mamá wailing at the loss of her mother each time someone put an arm around her. Delia huddled in a corner with María Elena, who was then nine years old, and their cousins. They cried on cue every time a grownup started to weep. Delia remembered smiling at María Elena to comfort her. But María Elena became angry.

"What are you laughing about! This isn't a party. *Abuelita* is dead! You don't feel anything, do you?" She slapped Delia across the face.

Their cousins stopped crying and stared, they looked shocked by María Elena's fury.

Delia rubbed her stinging cheek. "Yes, I am sad, too! And I'll tell Mamá you hit me!"

That was the first time María Elena had threatened to kill her-self if Delia told on her.

Delia turned around on the sofa to face the wall when she heard Papá locking the gate outside. She bit her lip until she tasted blood. She wished that the day had ended when Isabel and Justo took Toñito from her arms because they were going away on their hon-eymoon. Then everyone had cheered, whistled, applauded. Ana had cried happy tears again. Justo looked proud and Isabel had looked radiant.

Outside, the chains that suspended the hammock rattled as Papá sat and began swinging slowly.

Simmering.

Oh, how she longed to go to him to give comfort and to be comforted.

"The mother of my mother, the mother of the mother of my mother . . ."

Chapter 4

Delia avoided Papá's printing shop during the two weeks following Justo and Isabel's wedding. She busied herself with school work, but it was the discussion she overheard the night after the Salazar's wedding reception that kept her away. She knew she could not question Papá about it, regardless of how much closer she was to him than to Mamá. She sensed behind that incident were *cosas de gente grande*, which she was not supposed to know.

Papá seemed too busy to notice Delia's absence in the shop. Brother Cristóbal had sent two apprentices from the Arts and Crafts Institute in the parish to assist *Don* Ignacio during Justo's vacation and they seemed to take up a great deal of his time.

Papá's patience wore thin. Delia overheard a conversation he had with Mamá out in the patio, while Mamá gathered mangos to make *dulce* and Papá cut down spent vegetable plants to make room for a new crop.

"I swear to you, Berta, Carlos and Manuel can't keep their mind on their work. Their antenna is tuned to the scent of women and it starts to send out sparks with each *criada* who walks by on her way to the market. They trip over each other when a young woman walks in the shop," Papá had said.

One morning Papá was missing at the breakfast table.

"I'll wait for Papá before I eat," Delia had said when Mamá started to serve her.

"He's already left, *hija*." Mamá dished out scrambled eggs for herself and Delia. "He had to take care of some business early this morning."

Mamá and María Elena looked at each other, as they often did, as if no one else existed beyond the invisible circle that enclosed them and Delia felt locked out from an important event.

María Elena lowered her eyes quickly and spooned up some steaming oatmeal. Her hand trembled.

Delia's stomach did somersaults. She toyed with her scrambled eggs until María Elena finished her breakfast and left the table.

"Your food is getting cold," Mamá said, reaching to pat Delia's hand.

Delia put her fork down and looked directly into Mama's almond-shaped eyes, the color of strong coffee. Mamá lowered them, but not soon enough. Delia saw worry reflected in them.

"Mamá, I want to know what Papá is doing today. He doesn't open the shop this early . . ."

Doña Berta frowned and closed her eyes as if her daughter's words pained her. She sighed and shook her head.

"You are always so curious, *hija*. There are things you are too young to know. Someday, maybe, you will understand. But not now. *Son cosas de gente grande.*"

Mamá's eyes remained closed, her soft eyelashes resting over her high cheekbones like a curtain drawn against everything that surrounded her, including her daughter.

Delia had heard it too many times. "Grownup stuff" meant Mamá would not tell her anything because Delia was to be protected from events she was considered too young to handle.

She pushed away her plate and her chair scraped against the floor tiles when she stood up to leave. At the door, she turned to look at Mamá, whose elbows now leaned on the table. Her hands, joined at the fingertips, covered her mouth. She seemed to be praying.

Dinner was delayed that evening. Juliana had told Delia that Papá had called and left word that he would be about an hour late coming home.

Delia and María Elena had been in the *sala* listening to the radio and doing homework. When Delia finished hers, she stepped outside and looked past the entry gate. Papá's car wasn't among those rolling down the street.

Two small boys in short pants carried their shoes in their hands and jumped back and forth between the gutter and the sidewalk, splashing rain water. They reminded Delia of the birds that fluttered in the birdbath near the kitchen window.

A brightly painted bus loaded with workers on their way home for the day, leaned to one side when it rounded the nearby corner. The driver stuck his head out the window, honked several times, motioned to the boys, and yelled at them to get out of his way.

"*¡Tu mama!*" shouted back the older boy, while the younger one contented himself with raising his arms and waving at the passengers.

Delia smiled, admiring their defiance.

She stretched out in the hammock and watched the clouds, still swollen with rain, drifting above in the darkening sky. The parakeets in a nearby cage conversed and the sweet scent of the lemon tree heavy with blossoms mixed with the smell of damp earth and filled every corner of the patio. That, and the slow swing of the hammock, relaxed her.

Delia had dozed off and woke up when Papá arrived and the gate hasp jangled. She stopped the hammock's movement with one foot and sat up.

Papá threw her a kiss. He held a large white envelope under his arm.

Delia waved, but didn't follow him. The window behind the hammock was open and not too far away from where Mamá and Juliana were setting the table.

When Papá walked in, the radio in the *sala* went off.

"I had begun to worry, Nacho. How did it go?" Mamá said.

"Well, *mi amor*." He paused and Delia knew he was kissing her mother's lips in his own gentle way, as he did every time when he came home.

"We'll talk later," Papá said, "I'll change clothes and will be right back." Papá's voice deepened and he growled, "I am so hungry, I can eat a whole cow!"

Delia heard his footsteps on the stairs. She had already left the hammock when she heard Mamá calling her. She didn't respond.

Upstairs, Delia waited until her father closed the door in the hallway bathroom. Then she stepped into her parents' bedroom. The large white envelope was on the bed next to Papá's necktie. Her throat tightened when she read the printed letterhead: "Pablo Luis Morán, Attorney-at-Law," followed by an address.

Delia knew that area. It was not too far from her school and within a block from the Hall of Justice. She didn't need to see more. The name on the envelope linked it to the man who stood in the way of María Elena's adoption. The length of the envelope meant it contained legal papers.

She stepped out of the room and only slowed down when she reached the entry to the dining room. While she washed her hands at the kitchen sink, she wondered if she would be able to swallow food.

Juliana brought steaming casseroles and set them on the dining table in front of *Doña* Berta, who served portions to her family, as they handed her their plates.

Delia noticed that Mamá didn't seem tense anymore. Since Papá had arrived, her attitude had changed. She sounded cheerful.

"How soon can I start with Nena's school uniforms, Nacho?" Mamá asked, looking at him, while she reached for the plate María Elena handed her across the table.

"Right away, *mi amor*," Papá said, smiling at María Elena, who returned his smile with one of her own.

When she saw Delia looking at her, María Elena stuck out her chin, as if to say, "So, there!"

Delia made mental notes: María Elena had been accepted at the nun's high school. She would be rubbing elbows with girls from prominent families whose names could be traced back to the time of the *Conquista*. The white envelope Papá had carried contained the documents that made it possible for María Elena to receive a good education. Pablo Luis Morán had given her away. Papá would pay the high tuition. María Elena was legitimate in the eyes of God and of men, according to what Brother Cristóbal had said, but that still didn't make María Elena fully her sister, or did it? In God's eyes? Could she bring that up at confession?

Delia felt a tremor run through her, numbing her. She kicked off her shoes and flexed her toes hard, until she heard the joints pop. She took a sip of iced tamarind water and looked around the table over the rim of her glass. No one looked at her. Papá, Mamá, and

María Elena were busy with their food, but an invisible cord linked them, forming a triangle that left Delia out.

There was no other mention of María Elena's schooling during the rest of the dinner hour, but the mood was almost euphoric and Delia was brought up from the depths of her ruminations.

"Ana brought Toñito today, Nacho," Mamá said. "He's such a sweet baby. She just can't keep her eyes off him. She adores him! Isabel is going back to work soon and Ana will have him all day. I don't know how she'll manage that and the laundering."

"Ana won't have to take in laundry anymore, Berta," Papá said.

"Oh . . . ?" Mamá's inclined head questioned Papá.

"Beto has started to work as an assistant in the Customs building when he is not busy with his thesis," Papá said.

"That's good, Nacho. Did you help him get hired?"

"The job was already there, they just needed to find the right person to fill the position. It was only a matter of placing a phone call to the right boss," Papá said, buttering a small baguette.

"Will he have time to finish his thesis?"

"Yes, *mi amor*. It's a part-time job. But it pays enough."

Papá spooned the last of the *caldo* in his soup plate. Then, he added another bit of news.

"Isabel won't be going back to work. Justo got a raise," Papá said, cutting a piece of *bistec*. He pierced it with his fork, dipped it in savory tomato sauce and chewed it, looking at Mamá as if he had just presented her with a gift.

Mamá's eyes opened wide. She gulped down some of her tamarind water. "You didn't tell me you planned to do that!"

"I wanted to surprise you, *mi amor*."

Papá's nonchalant air didn't quite cover up his pleasure at Mamá's reaction. "I depend on Justo quite a lot now. I didn't realize until the past year and a half what a difference it would make to have good full-time help. He'll be earning enough now, so that Isabel can stay home and be the lady of the house, as it should be."

"Nacho, this is such a special day for me, *mi vida*, you've made things happen . . ." Mamá glanced at María Elena and there was laughter in Mamá's eyes. Then her eyes moved to Delia, whose look begged Mamá to say more.

Mamá did say more, but not what Delia wanted to hear. She didn't speak about María Elena or the adoption. Instead she asked, "Don't you think that's wonderful, Delia? Isabel will be able to stay at home and care for Toñito. She'll be the lady of the house, like every woman should be."

"That's good, Mamá," Delia said, "but maybe she'll miss her job. She liked dealing with people at the pharmacy."

Papá assumed a serious tone and settled the matter. "A married woman with a child belongs at home, like your Mamá, like my *madrecita,* God rest her soul. That's the way it is, *querida.*"

There was no point arguing with Papá. After all, Delia had started to notice that his point of view changed, depending on how close to him were those involved in an issue. The man who had promised to kick out of his house and disown any daughter who let a man take advantage of her sang a different tune where Isabel was concerned.

It seemed to Delia that the more she thought she understood grownups, the more confused she became.

After dinner, she joined María Elena in the *sala* and quietly helped put together a jigsaw puzzle. She didn't bring up the matter of María Elena's schooling. She sensed that subject, with the issue of her sister's legitimacy at the core of it, was too thorny to be safe. She was disappointed when Mamá and Papá took their coffee out to the porch. She felt María Elena's eyes on her and knew that the conversation between Mamá and Papá would remain private.

Chapter 5

Don Ignacio Pineda's life became less hectic with Justo's return to the shop. At home, Mamá and Juliana prepared for Easter, the time for the Pineda's last vacation trip before the new school term began.

Delia and her family would spend Semana Santa at their *hacienda* in the interior beginning on Palm Sunday and would return to the city the week after Easter. It was a time to join their friends and relatives and catch up with events in their lives. It was also a time to observe and participate in the Church's staging of the Passion of Christ with its nightly processions of *penitentes* lugging *pasos*, the decorated platforms featuring statues of Mary and Mary Magdalene, and Christ bearing on his shoulders the cross to Calvary. On Good Friday, the procession included the Stations of the Cross and the body of Christ in a glass coffin shouldered by men who had promised this humble service in exchange for miracles.

During Semana Santa, Delia was exposed to lives on the opposite extreme of her own family's in the city. Indian families came down from the mountains and staked their temporary claim on the grounds in back of the Pineda's *hacienda* by tying their horses to the fence posts and unrolling their sleeping mats on any available space.

The Pineda's backyard became a swarming world where women cooked in earthen pots over small fires, exposed their brown breasts to nurse babies, braided each other's hair, wrapped and unwrapped bundles, fed and watered the horses.

The men ate, sharpened machetes and cock spurs, bet at the cockfights, drank *guarapo* of fermented sugar cane, sang *mejoranas*, bluffed, argued and, sometimes, cut each other during drunken fights—usually over a woman.

Mamá and Papá became *padrinos* to countless Indian babies brought to town by their parents from the mountains on foot or horseback. They consecrated the babies to God in the mass baptisms that Father Domingo held at the centuries-old cathedral on Easter Sunday.

Papá would hand each couple a few Balboas as a gift for the child. These baptisms lacked the elaborate celebrations that usually followed individual baptisms in the city, but the look of reverent submission on the faces of the parents was celebration enough for Delia.

The Indians made semiannual treks to town. They also came down from the mountains at Christmas and at both times they combined religion and commerce. During their stay, they traded, worshiped, got drunk, and fornicated. Then they traveled back to their homes with new supplies, their souls at peace with God; their thoughts blurred, hung over from drinking binges; many of the women carrying new seed to be baptized the following year. Their passing left temporary footprints on dusty paths before tropical downpours washed them away, sealing the *campesinos'* lives within the confines of dense jungle growth, or plantations of bananas, coffee, sugar cane.

Delia saw Holy Week with mixed feelings. She enjoyed sitting with María Elena and their cousins on the low whitewashed wall that surrounded the *hacienda*'s house. They ate shaved ice, soaked with flavored syrup and topped with sweet condensed milk, to keep cool in the oppressive summer heat, and watched the parade of city dwellers who made the annual pilgrimage to the interior. They took in the drama of Christ's passion and resurrection as it unfolded with the participants displaying unquestionable devotion and excess.

Delia, María Elena, and the other young pilgrims followed the procession every night. They held flickering candles and sang hymns of supplication and praise. They formed a mysterious cortege wrapped in dust, smoke from torches, and the odor of sweat and burning wax. They made the required stops in front of selected homes to pray a rosary, sing canticles, or recite the beatitudes.

Delia had seen the spectacle for as long as she could remember. She was now twelve years old and her awe still turned to fear when she saw the penitents, dressed in simple purple gowns held at the waist with hemp ropes, carrying heavy, rough wooden crosses or walking the procession on bleeding knees over cobblestones and gravel. Her heart dropped into a sudden vacuum at the sight of flagellants who wept silently as they hit their own bare backs with leather or rope whips to which they had tied sharp pieces of metal or broken glass. Sweat and blood mixed and dripped down their backs like rivulets of repentance.

What wretched sins had these poor devils committed that qualified them for such harsh self-imposed penances? Delia wondered. Did God demand this extreme torment in exchange for his forgiveness, his grace? Hadn't Christ already paid that price for the redemption of all sinners?

In the cathedral, the bells stopped calling the faithful to mass during Holy Week. Instead, the Pinedas went to Mass responding to the call to worship from the sacristan who walked the streets shaking a rusted metal hasp nailed to an old wooden board.

The same board year after year; the same flat, joyless, monotonous clatter. That's how far the pall of sorrow reached into the town and its people.

The bells rang again at dawn on Domingo de Pascua de Resurrección, calling the congregation to the Mass of Resurrection on Easter Sunday. It was the end of death and mourning. It was the beginning of the celebration of life.

By the time the Pinedas joined the other believers and entered the holy temple on Easter Sunday, the mourning shrouds were off the altar and the alcoves where images of saints and apostles reflected the light of votive candles burning at their feet.

Delia took in the festive displays of white cala lilies and white roses that decorated the *altar mayor* and the rest of the church, manifesting the image of the church as the bride of Christ. She knelt on worn crimson velvet and felt sadness sliding away from her. It had been with her since Maundy Thursday when the priest had recited the Stations of the Cross.

Now, Father Domingo and his acolytes had shed their somber mourning vestments and donned white, gold and red embroidered robes edged with lace made by the hands of nuns in the seclusion of their convents. The sounds from the organ reverberated in the sanctuary as if trying to burst past the stained glass of the cupola to reach the heavens praising the glory of the Resurrection.

After the mass, the young people mingled about the plaza, all abuzz about that evening's dance in the Town Hall. Delia and María Elena joined them in the traditional walk around the sidewalk that surrounded the plaza. Boys and girls walked in opposite directions and met face-to-face. Strangers glanced at each other, some smiled. Those who were well acquainted joked or arranged further meetings.

Mamá and Papá served brunch at the *hacienda* for their relatives, their friends, and for Father Domingo.

The way that Papá included the clergy in his everyday life, wherever he might be, lifted him higher in Delia's esteem. Papá knew not only who possessed acumen about right and wrong, but, in her understanding, who had closer connections to Heaven's gatekeeper.

Mid-afternoon that Sunday, Papá had gone to the cockfights and Mamá and her childhood friend Otilia sat rocking on the front porch of the *hacienda* drinking pineapple coolers.

María Elena had asked Delia to come along for a swim in the river with friends, but Delia had declined. María Elena was a good swimmer and she would be showing off, diving from the high branches of the ceiba tree. Besides, Delia knew Mamá's meetings with Otilia always brought forth revelations about *cosas de gente grande*. The women took advantage of their reunions to update each other about current events in their lives. They often rehashed their family histories as if reminiscing reinforced their bond and validated their memories.

Delia sat cross-legged on the dirt, leaning her back on the other side of the low whitewashed wall that surrounded the house. She sat far enough from Mamá and Otilia so she wouldn't be noticed, but close enough to hear their conversation.

In the hot, windless summer day, Delia's sleeveless cotton dress stuck to her. She licked the last bit from a melting fruit bar and buried the stick in the soft dirt. For a while, she watched a row of red ants carrying chunks of green leaves larger than they, like a parade of sailboats with large green sails on their way to the horizon. The ants followed a path of their own making a short distance from her feet and disappeared into a hole in the ground.

The charms on Otilia's bracelet jingled. The straw fan she used to cool herself made a swishy sound, but when she spoke her basso overpowered the other noises. Besides, the women believed they were alone, there was no need for whispers.

"Nacho told me that Pablo finally saw reason. So many years, Berta, and that *sinverguenza* holding back just to make your life difficult. I can't understand why he has carried his selfishness this far."

When they were together, Mamá and Otilia dispensed with preambles. Their conversations seemed to start where they had left off, no matter how long ago. This time it would be no different.

Ice fell from a pitcher into a glass as Mamá poured more refreshment.

"Yes. He signed the adoption papers. María Elena will start school at Immaculate Conception with the new term," Mamá said. Then she raised her voice, spewing anger and old hate. "That man is a *desgraciado*! He really didn't care about Nena. He just wanted to make things difficult for me. He never forgave me for marrying Nacho. I still don't know what drove me to be so blind about that man," Mamá said.

"Don't punish yourself over it any more, Berta. Everyone makes mistakes. He took advantage of your innocence," Otilia tried to appease Mamá.

Delia wished that Otilia would lose the bracelet. The constant clinking of the charms annoyed her.

When Otilia spoke again, her voice had the lazy monotone of a litany, reminiscing.

"I can remember how excited you were when you got that job as court reporter. You wanted to be a career woman. Then Pablo came along wearing expensive suits, carrying his alligator skin briefcase and talking about how influential he was with the higher ups in government." Reproach and disdain colored Otilia's tone. "It never occurred to me that you would fall for such an arrogant man,

Berta! All he had to do was lay that Panama hat of his on your desk. It was like a dog marking his territory!"

Delia remembered the name on the large envelope she had seen Papá carry into their home some weeks ago. The man Mamá and Otilia were talking about was named Pablo Luis Morán and he had left in Mamá wounds that wouldn't heal and María Elena was one of them.

"I was eighteen, Oti. So naive . . ." Mamá's anger hadn't diminished.

The women were quiet for a moment. Then Mamá spoke again and Delia's heart beat a *rataplán* in tune with the sound of her mother's voice. Mamá's familiar restraint had ceased completely and she opened wide the gate of her emotions. The words that tumbled out frightened Delia, but she heard them all.

"That man lit a flame in me with a heat I had never felt before. His lust was fierce. It wrapped itself around me, choking me. I was so afraid of the feelings he unleashed in me, Oti, but I couldn't push him away. I knew I was being sucked into a forbidden whirlpool and I felt helpless. We couldn't keep our hands off each other. He showed me Heaven and Hell all at the same time. He made promises! I wanted him so much!"

"At a time like that, when men know you've fallen for them, they make all sorts of promises that don't mean a thing," Otilia said.

Mamá ignored the interruption and went on, unburdening the load she had carried for fourteen years. Her voice had the urgency of someone seizing the moment of a lifetime to confess sins that can't be forgiven beyond the grave.

"Once he took my innocence, I felt I had nothing left to offer any other man. And when I felt his child stir inside me, it wasn't bliss. It was the curse of Eve our mothers talked about. But when he offered to set me up in a *casa chica,* I spat on his face!" Mamá's sorrow subdued her somewhat and she sniffled. "I'll never forget the shame I brought to *mis viejos*. My Mamita cried for days and Papi wanted to kill him, remember?" She paused.

Waiting for Otilia to agree?

"Those were the most miserable nine months of my life. The difficult pregnancy, the guilt. If this was love, I never wanted it anymore."

"But then you would have missed Nacho and the life you have now," Otilia said.

Mamá let that pass. "I was lucky that Mamita and Papito sent me here instead of Papito carrying out his promise to throw me out of the house if I ever gave a man what that man had not earned by putting a ring on my finger."

So, *Abuelito* had said it too. Delia concluded that the threat of disownment was part of her family legacy. Like a surname: Delia Susana Pineda You-mess-up-with-a-man-you're-out-of-here.

Delia heard Mamá's deep sigh. She sighed, too, but it wasn't relief that she felt. Instead, she wanted to flee and couldn't.

"I wish they had lived long enough to see my daughter of shame become a legitimate daughter to Nacho," Mamá continued, "but he kept his promise to them. I couldn't wish for more, Oti."

Otilia's bracelets jingled again. She must have touched Mamá's hand, or her arm.

"Don't torment yourself anymore, Berta. My *mamá* was glad to be of help. She said that the birth was one of the more difficult ones she's had as a midwife, but worth it all."

Would Otilia's words be enough absolution for Mamá?

The drum solo that Delia's arteries were playing, reverberating in her head, became frantic. She tried to calm down when she heard Otilia's voice again.

"Ah . . . ! Women live their lives under the thumb of one man or another. The father, the lover, the husband, the son. The priest that won't marry you because the man you love is divorced."

"I know, Oti, it's like with you and Esteban."

"I wouldn't be his *querida*," Otilia said. "And he knew that. He didn't even ask me. I wouldn't bring that shame to *mis viejos*. But I still love him. I could never love another man and he knows that. But we'll never be together."

Otilia went on, as if checking items off a list. The summary of her life.

"So here I am, caring for my old folks, a make-believe aunt to my friend's children, running the ranch. Most men around here can't understand a woman who chooses to stand on her own. Their upbringing tells them that's impossible. Some of my friends' husbands approach me, as if by offering me a crumb of their life I should feel honored. One of them had the gall to call me a *macha* after I refused him. If I had accommodated him, he would have thought me a *puta*. He has high standards, you see?" Otilia spat out the last sentence.

"Yes, I understand," Mamá said. She was silent for a moment. When she spoke again, her question sounded rehearsed, as if she had pondered it for years.

"But, about Nacho . . . Do you ever have regrets, Oti?"

"Regrets?" The ice in Otilia's glass clinked again and again, like crystal chimes played by the wind. She must have been swirling it with her finger, as she often did.

Delia's eyes felt like burning coals in their sockets. They were dry, wide open. She blinked several times to relax and moisten them. Then she closed them and took deep breaths. The heat and humidity, the women's conversation, the weight of what their words unveiled, oppressed her.

"Do you regret introducing us? He could have married you," Mamá said.

Delia cringed. This was too much. Yet, she stayed to hear more.

"No. No regrets, Berta. I know Nacho too well. I love him like a brother."

Delia heard Otilia's chuckle.

"Marrying him would have been close to incest!"

The women laughed and their sad memories flew away, like doves startled by the sound of their laughter.

Delia's buttocks had grown numb. She hadn't shifted her position for fear Mamá or Otilia would notice her proximity. She had seen several ants walk over her toes. Her throat felt parched. She braced herself on her hands and raised herself off the ground a bit, bowing her aching head to remain out of sight beyond the wall. When she lowered herself again, a sharp pebble stabbed her.

The drumbeat in her head intensified. Delia clenched her teeth.

"Have you wondered all these years?" Otilia's bracelet dinged against the glass pitcher.

Another round.

Delia licked her dried lips when she heard ice and liquid being poured.

"Sometimes," Mamá's voice was calm now.

"Those were wasted thoughts, *amiga*," Otilia said. "You were meant for each other. Nacho is one of those rare men whose manhood is not measured by the amount of women he deflowers."

Delia wanted to run away now. Otilia was saying things about Papá that were too foreign. She knew what the words meant, but could not put them together with Papá in the same thought. In her mind, measuring Papá against other men diminished him.

"He has a quiet dignity. He is loyal. There is nothing superficial or arrogant about Nacho. You needed a real man in your life and I knew that he could see past the baby in your arms and love you," Otilia said.

Yes, Papá loved Mamá, notwithstanding María Elena.

"The man has been crazy about you from the moment he first saw you, Berta! He didn't see a woman with a fatherless child when he met you; he saw a beautiful, intelligent, charming woman. By the time you told him about María Elena, he didn't care. He has enough love for everyone."

"I only wish I could return love in the same way; but I still see Pablo's face behind my eyelids when Nacho takes me late at night. Forbidden love is a curse. It stays with you forever," Mamá said, then her tone became wistful. "You know, Oti, I've wished so many times that Delia had been a boy. It would have been nice if I had given Nacho a son."

All this was more grownup stuff than she could handle and a monstrous invisible weight pressed down on Delia's shoulders. She crawled away along the wall, her hands and knees feeling every particle of dirt, every sharp stone. Towards the back of the house, she stood up and leaned against the trunk of a palm tree and wept.

She had joined the Holy Week penitents. She had embraced a personal Calvary.

Chapter 6

"Stand still, Nena, or you'll get stabbed with a pin!" Mamá said.

María Elena squirmed constantly while she was being fitted with new school uniforms. Mamá lifted her arm and wiped the sweat off her forehead on the sleeve of her dress.

Delia stood next to Mamá and handed her the pins, one-by-one. Mamá was not one of those seamstresses who held pins between her lips and she disliked the wrist pincushion. "Too much like a factory worker," she had said. But she would not delegate the sewing of her daughters' clothes to anyone else. And, to Delia's despair, she made them to last. Once Mamá made her a dress, Delia was stuck with it until she outgrew it.

Two years had passed. María Elena, now fifteen-and-a-half years old, prepared to start her sophomore year at the School of the Immaculate Conception of Mary. Mamá adjusted her uniforms, taking them in to accommodate a slimmer waist and letting them out at the bodice for her fuller bust.

Delia watched her sister's development with curiosity more than envy. She saw how much María Elena savored being a *señorita* now.

Since the morning she woke up to find blood on her nightgown and on her bedding, María Elena's ties to Mamá seemed to have grown stronger. Since then, she studied the details of her manners and posture and she asked Mamá about fabrics, perfumes, fashion. She clipped magazine articles about anything that had to do with beauty, etiquette, and style and pasted them in a scrapbook.

When her friends came over, María Elena shared the wisdom from her scrapbook and they posed and experimented with make-up while they talked about this or that boy, and threw around predictions about their future lives.

"You'll wish you were in my shoes," María Elena would tell her friends. "My husband will be wealthy, a man in control of everybody around him, a handsome man. He'll put himself and everything he has at my feet. He's going to love me like they do in the movies. He'll bring me serenades for my birthday and surround me with servants. Not only one, like Juliana, but several servants. I know who he is, but I won't tell you his name. Not yet," she teased.

Delia sat on her bed or on the floor observing, enjoying everything with amusement, but not really participating. She wasn't expected to join in. After all, María Elena had said once when Delia tried to express an opinion, "Oh, forget it! At thirteen Delia is still a little runt!"

This morning María Elena had tried different ways to comb her dark brown hair and asked Delia to pin it up for her. She looked in the mirror, pleased with the sophisticated look that resulted from the pile of curls on top of her head. She winced and her hazel eyes moved from her image in the mirror, to look at her sister.

Impatient with her sister's demands, Delia had inadvertently scraped María Elena's scalp with the tip of a hairpin.

"You do that again and you won't be going to the beach tonight!" María Elena had warned with a harsh look in her hazel eyes.

Delia had ceased to wonder about the color of her sister's eyes. She knew now that their differences came from María Elena's father. She had never seen him, but Papá's and Mama's eyes were dark brown and so were Delia's.

Since that day more than a year ago on Holy Week, when Mamá's past was revealed, Delia had locked Mama's secret in the most remote chamber of her mind. It was enough for her to know. She didn't need to stir waters that seemed calm and risk smearing her family with the muck that lay underneath.

Now, the two girls were eager to finish fitting María Elena's uniform. They had preparations to make with Juliana for that evening's gathering at Linda Vista beach. The moon would be full and the *fogatas* on the white sand would serve not just as the only other light, but to cook the *chorizos* and *carne asada*. Summer was ending. The school year had just began and Delia, María Elena and their friends would have one more celebration under the supervision of their parents or the *criadas* who came to do the cooking. Juliana would be going with them to cook and to chaperone.

After she finished helping Juliana and María Elena cube, season and skewer lean chunks of beef and pork, Delia left the house by the back door. She bent over and placed a small book on the ground, then reached for an orange off the tree that stood near the vegetable beds, peeled it and tossed the peelings on a pile of old plant cuttings. She collected the book, blew dust off its cover and closed the gate behind her.

When she arrived at the printing shop, Delia found Justo alone, cleaning one of the presses.

"Where's Papá?" she asked.

"He's delivering an order. He'll be back soon. Can I be of any help?" Justo said, wiping his hands on a stained cloth.

"No, thanks. I'll just sit by the window and read."

"What are you reading these days, *chiquilla*?" Justo leaned sideways to read the title of Delia's book. "Uh, oh. Gustavo Adolfo Bécquer, no less! The romantic Sevillano. Read it slowly, *muchachita*, there's much romance and passion in those verses." Justo pointed an index finger in a warning gesture.

Delia, perched comfortably on the window seat, smiled at Justo. There was that word again: passion. The crime of passion. The passion of Christ. The passion in the poet's words.

Pensive, she looked out beyond the wrought iron grille that covered the window. The usual cadre of boys gathered at the street corner. They varied in age from early teens to those already shaving or attempting to look older by carefully stroking the mere wisp of a mustache. She watched them as Lilia, one of María Elena's classmates, approached carrying a pair of roller skates, a light breeze playing with her skirt and the sun glinting off her tousled hair. The boys signaled to each other with smiles and raised eyebrows and one of them called to Lilia as she hurried past them.

"*Oye, mamacita*, the day didn't start until you opened your eyes. Then the sun came out to lick the honey from your lips. When do I get to be the sun, *mamacita* . . ." He followed her, whispering *piropos*.

The other boys whistled and yelled, *"¡Ay, mamacita!"*

"Look at this, Justo," Delia beckoned tilting her head. "Why do they do that? It's so silly!"

Justo joined Delia at the window.

"They're machos-in-training, Delia. Men have been doing that since the world began. They're showing off to their friends. But if Lilia stopped and confronted them, they would be so scared they would forget their own names."

"I'd like to see that," Delia laughed. "Lilia won't do it. She said she hates it when they follow her and whisper, but I don't see her crossing the street to get away from them."

Justo shook an ink-stained index finger at Delia. "You are perceptive, *chiquilla*. Now, the quiet boys, those are the ones you want to watch out for. They are past trying to prove themselves to their friends. When they approach a lady, they are serious. Like Alberto Guzmán. You see him?"

Justo pointed at one of the older boys. The tallest one, who leaned against the wall, his hands in his pockets, one leg bent, his foot propped against the wall, completely relaxed.

The Guzmán family owned the building where Justo and Isabel lived and Alberto often took Toñito to the park to teach him how to pitch a baseball. At seventeen, and in his senior year at the public school, Alberto was often the subject of conversation among María Elena's friends when they gathered in their room, but María Elena wasn't the one who brought up his name.

Delia saw Justo's friendly advice as ground where she could dig deeper.

"Is that passion, Justo?"

The question took Justo by surprise and he quickly turned to face her. He frowned. "What kind of question is that, *chiquilla*, what do you know about passion?"

Delia shrugged, but kept her eyes fixed on Justo's.

"Well, the priest said that Holy Week was about Jesus Christ's passion." She lowered her voice and ventured further. "You killed your wife for passion."

Justo's eyes widened. There was a wounded look in them. After a moment, he nodded. Sadness shadowed his face.

"You know too much, *chiquilla*," he said and turned to look at the boys standing at the street corner. One of them was buying a fresh coconut from a street vendor, who chopped a piece off the fruit with a machete, punctured the soft shell and stuck a drinking straw in it.

Justo watched the vendor pushing his cart down the street until the man disappeared from view. When he faced Delia, his eyes were moist.

Remorse gnawed at her. Justo had never done anything to hurt her. On the contrary, he had become a good friend, one with whom she could be as open as she was with Papá. Now she wished she could take back her words. Her remark about Justo's past had been unkind. She bit her lower lip. How could she tell him how sorry she was?

"Look, Delia, there are different kinds of passion. Passion is an overpowering feeling. It can be an obsession. It can be a suffering so intense that it makes you give all of yourself to it. Like our Lord's passion. His love for us has no limits. He suffered for us, so deeply. He died for our salvation. That's the noblest of passions, Delia. That passion is expressed with sacrifice and belongs to the saints."

Justo went to a nearby workbench, picked up a thermos bottle, pulled the cork, and poured hot coffee into a cup.

Delia watched him take a sip. He had allowed her to open a door into his thoughts and she waited quietly for him to say more, but her heart was beating faster.

Justo came back and sat next to her. Looking out the window, he continued, "There is the passion of jealousy that blinds you, blurs your thinking and destroys you and those around you. That passion is human. That passion is evil. It makes us do horrible things that we later regret, but never forget."

While he spoke about the passion of Christ, Justo's voice had been reverent. When he spoke about jealousy as a passion, his voice filled with sorrow that invaded Delia with each word that he uttered.

"That passion is what feeds crimes, even against those that we love. It eats at you." His fist went to his chest. "It leaves a hole in your soul that can't be filled with penance. It reminds you that, no matter how many other things you do right in your life, the day your life ends, when you meet God, you'll still owe him an explanation."

The sun coming through the window glinted on the tears suspended on Justo's eyelids and Delia could not look at him anymore. She lowered her eyes and looked at the book she held in her hands.

He was talking about his passion. The passion that blinded him and robbed him of ten years of his life. His voice had betrayed his agony. His marriage to Isabel and the love he poured on her and their son had not erased his sorrow or lightened the weight of the cross of guilt he would carry forever.

They were quiet for a moment.

When Delia looked at him again, Justo nodded and went on, this time with a lighter tone. "There is the passion that focuses all the attention of a person. Like the compulsion that drives collectors to gather things around them: silver, paintings, books . . ."

Justo placed his hand on Delia's shoulder. "You may fall prey to that passion, *chiquilla*, the way you keep asking your Papá for new books." He pinched Delia's nose gently. "You can see a lot if you get your nose out of the books once in a while, *chiquilla*."

"I see plenty. More than you think. Tell me more about passion."

"There is the passion in the poet's verses. The passion that fills you with joy, that makes your heart beat so fast and so loudly, like the drums of a *tamborito* on Fat Tuesday. You can't hear anything else, but the songs of the birds, the crash of the ocean waves on the shore, the rustle of the wind caressing tree leaves. The music in the words of the one you love is like timpani and violins playing all at once. That passion is love and it makes your soul sing. You'll want it to last forever."

Delia could hardly keep up with Justo's description. It was all too full of feelings. She saw Justo as a man whose passion could give life. Or death. It frightened her that passion could be so powerful. If it had driven Justo to commit such a hideous murder, how had he expressed the depth of his love? How tender had his touch been? How sweet his kisses? How loud did his soul sing? She felt blood rush to her face and tried to swallow the lump that stuck in her throat.

Justo must have noticed, because he fell silent, took the book from her hands, opened it at random and read to her softly:

> *Podrá nublarse el sol eternamente;*
> *podrá secarse en un instante el mar;*
> *podrá romperse el eje de la tierra*
> *como un débil cristal.*
>
> *¡Todo sucederá! Podrá la muerte*
> *cubrirme con su fúnebre crespón;*
> *pero jamás en mí podrá apagarse*
> *la llama de tu amor.*

Justo closed the book, placed it between Delia's hands and held her hands together.

"That passion, *chiquilla*, is the passion I wish for you. When you are older, when you become a woman, I wish for you, that a man will love you like the poet loves. That he will say to you:

> *The sun may cloud up eternally;*
> *the sea may dry in one instant;*
> *the axis of the earth may break*
> *like a fragile crystal.*
>
> *All that may happen!*
> *Death may cover me*
> *with its funeral crepe;*
> *but nothing will ever*
> *dim in me love's flame."*

Delia freed her hands, and hugged him. She wanted to cry, but didn't. They held each other for a moment, he with his sad memories, she with her new awareness.

"Trying to steal my girl, are you?"

It was Papá. He had come in unnoticed through the back door of the shop and Delia wondered if he had heard their conversation.

He handed her a small paper bag. "Here, *querida*, indulge one of your passions."

She was happy instantly. She knew the bag contained Perugina chocolates, Papá's special treat for her.

Not one to waste a mood, Delia asked, "Did you ever wish I was boy, Papá?"

"Of course not! And have you standing on the street corner waiting for some girl to walk by so you can spit in her ear, like those boys do?" His thumb indicated the group of boys outside. "Never! You give me too much pleasure, *querida*, just as you are." He kissed the top of Delia's head.

Papá clapped his hands as if to break a spell. "Well, Justo, are we going to stand here and let Delia distract us, or are we going to be printers?"

Justo Salazar and *Don* Nacho Pineda busied themselves with their work. Delia bit into a chocolate nougat and turned to look at the boys standing at the corner.

Alberto Guzmán would be at the beach party that evening. María Elena had said so when she spoke to Isabel on the phone shortly before Mamá called them to fit the uniforms.

Although he looked relaxed today, Delia had seen Alberto in action at the street corner more than once. He was the star of his school's soccer team and had a knack for suggestive *piropos*, the compliments that young men aimed at the girls as they walked by their sidewalk gatherings. But he didn't follow behind for a half a block or so whispering like the others did. So, if Justo was right, Alberto Guzmán could mean passion.

The sun had already set when Papá helped Juliana and the girls load the baskets of food into the trunk of his Ford sedan and then drove them to Linda Vista beach.

"I'll be here at eleven thirty, Juliana. Have everything ready to go," he said when he shut the lid on the empty car trunk.

"But Papá, no one else leaves before midnight!" María Elena pleaded, following *Don* Nacho to the driver's door.

"Since when are my daughters everyone else? By midnight you and Delia will be at home, Nena. Now, help Juliana with those baskets." He turned on the ignition and left.

Delia followed María Elena's lead. She took off her sandals, carried them in one hand and slipped the handle of a basket on her other arm. She sunk her feet on the dry sand dunes, past swaying palm trees and mangrove growth, toward the bonfires that burned bright sending up sparks in the moonlight, then felt the cool, firm, wet sand as they approached the shore where a crowd of young people fanned the hot coals to keep ignited the driftwood of their *fogata*. The early arrivals had already stripped to their swimsuits or swimming trunks and some of them were dripping salty ocean water, their voices and their laughter mixing with the sound of the surf.

Soon after, Juliana placed skewered pieces of spicy marinated meat on a metal rack over the flames. Other adults spread blankets and secured them against the evening breeze, burying the corners in the sand. The Guzmáns had provided an ample supply of corn on the cob for roasting and others had brought salads, watermelons, mangos and pineapples. Galvanized tubs held ice and soft drinks for the teenagers and beer for the adults.

Alberto Guzmán sat on a towel spread on the sand, strummed a guitar and began to sing a bolero. The mellow, susurrant tone of his voice was soon echoed by others who sang with him the romantic lyrics:

> *Mujer, si puedes tu con Dios hablar*
> *Pregúntale si yo alguna vez*
> *Te he dejado de adorar . . .*

Delia joined in the singing. "Perfidia" was the perfect song for a moonlit night by the sea, a lover's lament.

> *Woman, if you can speak with God,*
> *ask him if at any time*
> *I have ceased to love you.*
> *And ask the sea,*
> *the mirror of my heart,*
> *how many times it has seen me cry*
> *the perfidy of your love . . .*

She and María Elena were peeling off the charred husks from roasted ears of corn when the music stopped. Delia looked up and saw Alberto hand the guitar to another boy and stand up.

Alberto stretched up his arms and arched his back. Behind him, a shaft of moonlight reflected on the water made a backdrop where Alberto's silhouette was outlined by the light of the *fogata*.

Delia realized he wasn't a boy anymore. The muscles on his torso rippled and tensed. The light and shadows from the *fogatas* played on the sinews of his legs covered with fine black hair and grains of sand.

María Elena stood up and Alberto glanced at her. She dropped the white shirt she had borrowed from Papá to wear over her green swimsuit, smiled at him and ran towards the surf. Seafoam splashed around her legs when she reached the water.

He followed.

Chapter 7

Ana gave her grandson, little Toñito, a small bicycle for his third birthday. Delia and María Elena often took him to the park where he could ride freely. Sometimes Ana went with them and sat on a bench reading romance novels in old *Vanidades* magazines given to her by her clients, or doing crochet, but always aware of Toñito's whereabouts. She dispensed comfort with a hug and a kiss when the child tumbled and soothed Toñito's wounds with a greenish ointment.

"What is that?" Delia had asked once, when she saw Ana dip her index finger in a small tin, make the sign of the cross over Toñito's scrape and gently rub the salve on it.

"Mostly aloe vera," Ana said. "Aloe is a miracle plant. My mother showed me how to extract it and mix it with other ingredients to make a healing salve."

Delia remembered the old gossip. Was this medicine the product of one of Ana's "gathering nights" as Juliana had called them?

"Where do you get that?"

"I grow the plant in a pot on my patio. Your mother has one too. I gave it to her. It's the one with the broken leaves. When you get a cut or a burn, or get an insect bite, you break a piece of the leaf and squeeze out the sap. It's a God-given healer, Delia, like many other plants."

This was a chance to find out more about the enigma that was Isabel's mother, and Delia wasn't about to waste the moment.

"Why did you make the sign of the cross on Toñito, Ana? Mamá never did that with us when we had cuts or scrapes."

"I do it so our Lord Jesus will bless the healing."

Delia's incredulous smile urged Ana to explain.

"Nothing is possible without him, *niña*. If you believe in him, he'll take care of you. When you cross yourself, you put yourself in his hands. So until Toñito learns, I'll do it for him."

"And do you have to break the leaves off the aloe vera at night, in the moonlight?" Delia prodded.

The old woman's wiry body shook. Her laughter rang loud, startling the birds in the trees. To Delia, Ana's glee didn't sound at all like a witch's cackle.

Ana pulled a clean white handkerchief from her pocket and dabbed at the tears in her eyes.

"You've heard that too, huh?"

"Uh-huh," Delia nodded, embarrassed. She had been caught tossing the bait.

"It isn't true, Delia."

"What is the truth then?" Delia insisted.

Ana leaned over and whispered, "I'll tell you the truth; but promise me you'll keep it to yourself. I like a little mystery in my life. You understand?"

Amused, Delia crossed her heart. "Promised!"

"My mother was a *curandera*. She was taught by her mulatto mother. She knew which plants were good for healing and which were poison. She knew how to mix a plaster that would bring down a fever, which leaves to burn so the smoke would keep insects at bay, which combination of herbs was good for a tea. She knew that to keep your hair thick and shiny there's nothing better than a rinse made of rosemary, thyme, eucalyptus, *manzanilla* and rose water."

Ana smoothed her salt and pepper hair with her hand.

"You see my hair? It will get all white some day. But it'll never fall off."

Like Isabel's hair, Delia thought, like Papá said, "a road to a man's perdition."

"Have you written down your recipes?" she asked.

"They haven't been written down, as far as I know," Ana said. "It's knowledge passed on for generations of mixed breeds: Africans, Spaniards, Indians. That's all. I am not a witch. Witches harm other people. Have you ever seen me harm anyone?"

Delia looked into the honest eyes of Isabel's mother.

"No. I'm sorry, Ana. But people say . . ." Delia shrugged. How would she get out of this one?

"So? Does that make it true? Don't listen to the *malas lenguas*, *niña*. It's a waste of your time," Ana said. She picked up the straw

bag that lay on the park bench next to her and put away the handkerchief and the tin with the ointment.

Delia watched her quietly and decided this was as good a time
as any to learn more about Ana. "But what about your headaches?"
she asked.

"They're headaches. What do you want me to tell you?"

Delia ignored the edge in Ana's voice.

"The asafetida patches you have behind your ears. Are they for
the headaches?"

"Yes," Ana sighed, "and you know something? They don't
work. Because the headaches I get are not from too much sun, or
from too much reading. They're not on my forehead. They're on
the top and the back of my head. And nothing stops them once
they start. They go away on their own after a while, or after a few
days."

"Have you seen a doctor?"

Ana looked heavenward. "Oh, yes, I've seen doctors and I've
seen *curanderos*."

Ana's response had the tired tone of someone who has exhaust-
ed all options.

"The *curanderos* want my money. They know they can't help
me. The doctors want to make a hole in my head and operate. But
I'll die before anyone takes a knife to me!"

Ana tightened her grip on her bag, holding it against her chest
like a shield.

"I was born whole. And I'll die whole. I'm not letting any doctor take me apart!" She punctuated her words with a firm nod.

Delia had heard other older men and women talk like that. She
didn't know if they were brave, or just plain cowards. She sensed
Ana's fear and opted to stop her inquisition. She promised herself
she would follow Ana's advice and stop listening to wagging
tongues.

Delia observed Ana's affectionate ways with Toñito. She had
seen the same dedication in other grandmothers. She and María
Elena had lost their last grandparent when Mama's mother had died
and Delia remembered very little about her. A lengthy illness had

kept *Abuela* bedridden, in a small bed in a small room that smelled of lemons and sour flesh, and unable to spend time with her grand-daughters. That was all Delia remembered: the smell and the moans and being kept away because *Abuela* needed peace and quiet.

Delia lacked information about Papá's and Mamá's parents. They were seldom mentioned at home in her presence, because Papá and Mamá tended to become sad and their reminiscences soon turned to renewed mourning, Mamá crying openly, "Why did they leave us, so soon! Oh, how I would like to have them here by me!" And Papá pulling out one of his monogrammed handkerchiefs and blowing his nose and wiping his eyes. "She was a saint! There will never be another woman in the world like my mother!" he lament-ed.

But now Delia needed to know more about her grandparents, what in her own life was affected by theirs, all tributaries merging in her being, forming her.

She wondered whose footsteps she would follow when she became a woman. Not Mamá's. Delia would not rely on men to direct her destiny, whatever that might turn out to be. She would never hide in shame to give birth to an illegitimate child like Mamá did. She would not marry a man because she was about to have his child, like Isabel did. Unlike María Elena, she wasn't planning to choose a husband for the material comforts she could get out of him.

Delia knew who she didn't want to be. She would have a say in her own future; but she thought that to begin shaping her future, she needed a base from which to build; and that base, she reasoned, had to start with her ancestors, her bloodline.

On this day, upon her return from the park, Delia looked up surveying the sky. Tropical winter clouds raced above Panama City, but withheld the downpour. The mugginess changed the landscape: Children stayed in the shade, playing jacks instead of jumping rope on the sidewalk; street vendors stopped meandering and stationed their carts under the shelter of huge rubber trees where they waited for customers. Even the lizards that often did pushups on the bricks that paved the walkway had taken shelter under the shade.

In the humidity, the fabric of her sleeveless print dress stuck to her, revealing the youthful form that had started to fill out in promising curves. She felt the weight of her wavy hair that hung loosely down to her waist, with a few curls pasting themselves on her forehead, punctuation marks for her thoughts. Her oval face, the mellow brown of cinnamon, tingled. She knew that if she were to look in a mirror at that moment, there would be rosy flames on her cheeks. She was aware of her body maturing and she responded to the sultry environment like a flower in a hothouse. Blooming.

When she saw Papá working in the garden, Delia uncoiled the water hose from a wooden hook attached to the wall that faced the Pinedas' patio. She took off her sandals, turned on the water and washed the dust off her feet. Then she splashed water on her face and her neck and walked towards Papá, holding the dripping hose. She stopped every so often to water a wilting plant and watched the thirsty earth suck up the moisture.

Mamá had sown cucumber seeds in small pots and they had sprouted quickly. Now Papá transplanted the seedlings to one of the raised beds, where Mamá and Juliana tended the vegetables that the servant cooked in so many different ways for the family.

Papá kneeled on the loose dirt and pressed down the soil around one of the tender seedlings.

"*Hola, querida*, you are on time to help me keep these babies from wilting. Sometimes I think your Mamá should go into business and open a sidewalk stand. I know we have too many vegetables growing here. Your mother is lucky that the neighbors help harvest the excess."

Delia placed her thumb on the end of the hose to let a gentle drip moisten the newly stirred ground.

"Mamá says that the vegetables she grows here are healthier than the ones they sell in the market."

"I know, *querida*. And she is right. Although the vegetables that went to the market from your *abuelo* Adan Pineda's farm were always the best," Papá said, stacking up several empty seed pots.

Papá pulled out his pack of cigarettes and a box of matches from the pocket of an old, faded green shirt that hung from a branch of a blooming cashew tree, then sat under the shade of the tree, his legs stretched before him, crossed at the ankles. Hunched over, he struck a match, cupped his hands around the flame and lit the cigarette. He blew out the match and placed it inside the matchbox. He would throw it away later. He leaned back against the tree trunk, blew a puff of smoke and closed his eyes.

Delia watched Papá rest, a feeling of calm but deep love invaded her as she inventoried this man of average height, without an ounce of fat on his body. He wore a white ribbed undershirt that left bare his hard and sinewy arms. Those arms lifted heavy reams of paper on and off the printing presses. Papá's hands, where dry bits of dirt remained, could swing a hammer with the same grace that they held Mama's hands when they talked, looking into each other's eyes. His ample forehead slanted towards the hairline of wavy, shiny black hair that he kept short and combed back without a part. The most prominent feature on his face was his slightly beaked nose. Papá suffered from allergies and Delia concluded that the shape of his nose had been affected by the constancy with which he blew it.

Papá took another drag from his cigarette and let the smoke drift out from his nose. It brought to mind pictures of raging bulls; but she knew better. There was no rage in Papá. He was a man at peace with his life.

Delia smiled when *Don* Nacho opened his eyes and saw her looking at him. If I were a boy, Delia thought, I know whose footsteps I would follow.

He beckoned her with a gesture. "That's enough water for now, *querida*. Come sit by me. The cashew blossoms smell good at this time of the day when the sun warms them."

Delia turned the faucet off at the wall and coiled the hose on a hook. Walking back, she brought her hair forward over her shoulder so it wouldn't get caught on the bark when she sat under the mango tree and faced Papá.

They would be alone for a while. Mamá was busy inside the house with Juliana and María Elena had gone to Isabel's house. Papá had time to rest. She had time to query him.

"Why did *Abuelo* sell his land to Otilia's family, Papá?"

"He wanted to move to the city."

"But he was a farmer. What would he do here?"

Papá took another drag from his cigarette. She waited until he blew smoke out again and watched it drift away. Then Papá turned to her.

"I had just finished high school and he didn't want me to board with relatives here while I went to the University. He wanted us to be together. Mamacita, him and me. So he sold his land in Cerro Pintado and rented some rooms near Santa Ana Plaza. We moved to the city and he began to work at the print shop, just like Justo does now."

"Who owned the print shop then?" Delia ran her fingers through the ends of her hair, slowly combing it, giving herself time to take in all this new information about her family.

"The Boyd family did. When old *Don* Emilio died, the family put the shop up for sale and your *abuelo* bought it. By then he had learned everything there was to know about making books and about the business. Things would have been so different, *querida*, if it had not been for the cursed influenza."

Papá closed his eyes. He drew a breath and licked his upper lip with the tip of his tongue. He had the habit of doing this when he pondered something difficult.

"Adan Pineda deserved a better death. Not just some lousy sudden illness . . ." he whispered.

Delia rushed another question lest Papá become sentimental.

"And how old were you then?"

"Twenty-two. Just one year short of graduation at the University. I was going to be a lawyer. I wanted to help people. Maybe go into politics later," Papá said, burying the rest of the cigarette in the dirt.

He looked at Delia. There was sadness in Papá's eyes, but no tears yet.

Merciless, she pressed on. "And then what, Papá, be president?"

Don Nacho chuckled. "Oh, no! My dreams were realistic. I dreamed that I could do more for our country in the National Assembly."

"Is that why you kept taking María Elena and me to watch the Assembly at work? Sometimes I got very bored, you know?"

"That's because you let your mind wander, *querida*. No, we went there for the same reason we go to the horse races, the basketball games, boxing matches, the theater, the museum. Because I want my daughters to know at least a little about everything. That way you can make choices later for your own life. About what you want to become, what you want to accomplish."

Papá glanced toward the house and assumed a confidential tone. "Between you and me, *querida*, cooking and sewing are fine. But a young woman these days can do much more than that. Who knows? Twenty years from now, *you* could run for president," Papá said, clicking his tongue and winking at Delia.

She smiled, then said, a bit defensively, "Mamá knows more than cooking and sewing. She could work outside and earn a living too, if she had to."

"I know that. She is a very smart woman. You learn a lot from her. But no wife of mine is going to work for a living. No, sir! No Pineda woman ever needed that!"

Papá's *machismo* and pride prevailed.

Delia kept him on track. "What happened after *Abuelo* died, Papá?"

"I had to take over, become the man of the house. *Mamacita* had only me then. She was *una mujer de su casa,* and the lady of the house relies on her men to provide."

"What did you do?"

"I knew the business well enough, because I helped my father when I wasn't studying. So I quit the University and took over the shop. I was twenty-three years old and I was a man responsible for a business, for my mother and for myself. Judith Pineda could be proud of her men. To the day she died, she never lacked anything."

Ignacio Pineda was proud of himself, his daughter thought.

Papá was growing pensive, but not tearful. He leaned his head against the trunk of the cashew tree and closed his eyes.

The late afternoon breeze played with the leaves on the fruit trees and moved around the aroma from ripening fruit. Above Delia, a family of hungry parakeet chicks raised a ruckus where they nested on the higher branches of the mango. As she looked up, she saw María Elena sitting on the second story balcony that surrounded the Pineda's patio. She had returned home and was drying her shoulder-length hair just as Isabel used to do, letting the rays of the afternoon sun caress it.

When Delia looked at Papá again his eyes were still closed. She brought him back.

"I know that *Abuelo*'s family was all born in Panamá, Papá. But *Abuela* was born in Spain, no?"

Papá opened his eyes. "If you toss me a mango, *querida*, we'll get back to history."

Delia stood up, gathered the skirt of her dress between her legs, climbed to one of the lower branches of the mango tree, and picked a fragrant ripe mango she tossed to Papá's waiting hands. She brought down another one for herself.

Just like Papá did, Delia wiped the dust off the red mango with her hands, bit off a piece of peel from its pointed end and spat it out. With her teeth, she held the edge of the bitten peel and pulled the mango away to bare the juicy flesh.

Papá swallowed and licked mango juice from the corners of his mouth.

"The Herreras came here when my mother was just four years old, and my uncle Miguel was two. They left Valencia and came to join friends who had bought land in Cerro Pintado and had written telling them how fertile the land was, and that everything grew here. Soon the Herreras owned land in Cerro Pintado and hired men to work their crops. My grandfather was among the workers. My father and my mother knew each other since they were children. The land where I was raised was my mother's dowry."

"*Abuela* was very beautiful," Delia said. The sepia-toned photograph of an elegant, fair-skinned woman was displayed under convex glass in an oval mahogany frame that hung on a wall in the Pineda's *sala*. She looked serene, her hair parted on the side with a blond wave falling over her forehead, her clear, direct eyes looking straight at the viewer, a gentle smile on her lips. Her delicate hands rested on her lap holding a small book.

Delia had heard Papá tell how, when he was twenty-five years old, *Abuela* developed terrible chest pains that kept her in bed for days at a time. One day she had looked up and asked him to bring her a glass of water. When he returned, she seemed to be sleeping. When he tried to wake her up, she didn't respond. Usually, it was at this point in the story when Papá pulled out his handkerchief.

To avoid sentiment that would snip the thread of confidence they were spinning, Delia rushed another question.

"But what made her a saint, Papá?"

Don Ignacio Pineda looked at his daughter, took a couple more bites of the mango. Then he spoke as if opening a curtain of years and feelings to let his daughter peek beyond.

"What makes a woman a saint, *querida*, comes through the man she marries. What she allows him, what she forgives him, what she denies herself on his behalf."

Delia ate some more of her mango. Papá seemed distant again and she pondered his words. In his eyes, Delia's grandmother seemed to have the attributes of a saint, to be sure; but was that all a woman could hope to be? She didn't see sainthood in any form as her own destiny. She had to know what her grandmother had allowed and forgiven to be held in such high regard by Papá. She felt poised on the edge of an emotional precipice but having stepped this far, she would not back from it. She pulled up her knees, rested her chin on them, and opened her arms, silently asking Papá to be forthcoming.

Papá finished his fruit, tossed the stringy stone into one of the empty seed pots and wiped his hands on the legs of his workpants.

"Adan Pineda was a lady's man. He kept a *casa chica*. *Mamacita* knew it and never reproached him. But I saw her suffering. It's not easy for anyone to share the love of their life. I swore I would never do that to my wife. It happens often. But having more than one woman is not what makes a man worthy. Being faithful to only one is the true test of a man's capacity to love, *querida*."

There was resentment in Papá's voice. And sadness as he looked toward the house. From the kitchen window came the murmur of Mama's voice talking to Juliana.

"Did you know Mamá before *Abuela* died, Papá?" Delia ventured, trying to piece loose ends now and Papá seemed to know it. His answer was guarded.

"I met your mother after that."

She cast her line again, trying to keep her voice from trembling. "How, Papá?"

When *Don* Ignacio looked at her, Delia lowered her eyes and bit her lower lip. Suddenly, all the noises seemed to stop: the parakeets' chatter, the wind on the leaves, her mother's voice in the distance.

Had she gone too far? Had she been too bold? She looked at her father as he stood up and extended a hand to help her stand. He put his arm around her shoulders and they began to walk toward the house, their heads inclined, matching steps.

"Otilia introduced us when your mother was spending some time with Otilia's family in the interior. It was soon after *Mamacita* had died and I was finishing some business in Cerro Pintado. When I first saw your Mamá, it was like meeting the other half of my soul. Her beauty took my breath away, her calm, sweet manner enchanted me. I knew we were destined for each other. Now close your question box, *querida*. Time for us to get cleaned up."

And the baby, Papá, what about the baby? That was a question Delia knew she dared not ask.

Papá seemed to have timed his answer, because they had reached the back door. The smell of roasting chicken and spicy beans wafted from the kitchen and they heard the clink of flatware as Juliana set the dinner table. Papá bent down to shake the dirt off the espadrilles he wore when he worked in the garden and above them, the clouds began to open up, large drops of rain splattering on the tiles outside the kitchen door.

Delia kissed his cheek quickly and went inside. She took the stairs two at a time, holding tight to the new piece to be fitted into the puzzle that was her life.

Chapter 8

Tap-tap-tap, tap-tap-tap . . .

Delia became more annoyed each time Mrs. Wells hit the edge of her desk with the ruler, keeping time with English verb conjugation. Of all days to have Mrs. Wells standing next to her, spitting out t's and p's, her breath reeking from ill-fitting dentures, alcohol, and stale tobacco, this was the very worst.

Delia held her arms tightly across her abdomen trying to still the cramps that had started at dawn and seemed to be getting worse. She had Mamá to thank for this.

Mamá had breezed into the girls' room that morning, with cheerful greetings for Delia.

"*¡Feliz cumpleaños, hija!* Tonight we'll celebrate."

"Maybe I should stay home, Mamá. My stomach hurts this morning." Delia had pulled the sheet up to her neck.

"It's only nerves. You become a *quinceañera* only once in your life. But this happens to be Friday and you will go to school. Besides, if you are around today, your birthday party will hold no surprises for you this evening," Mamá said when she handed a robe to Delia, urging her to get out of bed.

María Elena had gathered up her books and gently teased Delia, pulling her toe on her way out of their room.

"Fifteen years old, maybe. But still not a *señorita!*"

Mamá shot María Elena a warning look.

"Delia ignored the remark. After all, she was not supposed to know what María Elena meant. So what if it was so important to Mamá that she had taken Delia to see Dr. Cabrillo, just to be reassured that there was nothing wrong with her.

"Your mother thinks you need a checkup," Dr. Cabrilo had said and winked. "What do you think? Is it an ailment of your head or your heart?"

She shrugged.

"Let's check your heart, then."

61

She suppressed a giggle while he pressed the stethoscope to her back. They had played this game when she was a little girl. If she had a cough, he would check her toes and tickle her feet and declare her healed. Then, as if to humor her mother, he would examine her seriously and prescribe the necessary medication to treat the cough.

"Heart sounds fine to me," he said and they both laughed. He looked in her chart. "Fifteenth birthday coming up. Now, have you noticed anything unusual?"

She shook her head.

"Stomach cramps?"

"No, doctor."

He looked at her for a moment. "Anything you want to talk about?"

"I don't think so."

Outside the examining room, Delia overheard Dr. Cabrillo and Mamá talking.

"But she hasn't menstruated yet. María Elena started earlier," Mamá argued.

"It happens, Señora Pineda. Some girls don't start their period until they are sixteen. Give her time and stop worrying. Trust me. She's doing well. It'll happen soon enough. Then you can start worrying about keeping the boys away."

Delia looked again at the wall clock in the classroom.

Four minutes to go before class would be over.

She blinked when a small flame flew across her line of vision from the back of the classroom, landed at Mrs. Wells' feet and exploded.

The old *gringa* gasped. Her hand flew to her chest. She stepped back and fainted. Mrs. Wells' head thumped when it bounced against the leg of a desk.

At that same moment, warm, sticky moisture began to build up in Delia's underpants. She remained seated and watched in a daze as the other students ran to help Mrs. Wells, who lay motionless on the floor.

The explosion had swallowed all other sounds, leaving a loud buzzing inside Delia's head, a sulfurous smell that almost gagged her. People were coming and going.

Miss Camacho rushed in from the adjoining classroom and sent the kids out of Mrs. Wells' room.

Miss Camacho and Mrs. Wells seemed enveloped in a thin gray cloud and Miss Camacho didn't notice that Delia was still at her desk, holding both hands to her ears.

Mrs. Wells wasn't moving. Miss Camacho waited, holding the older woman's head on her lap, stroking her forehead, talking softly to her until ambulance attendants arrived and placed Mrs. Wells on a stretcher.

Before they carried her out, Miss Camacho pulled down the dress that had bunched up around the fallen woman's thighs. Delia saw that Mrs. Wells' clunky orthopedic shoes pointed up and out. One of them had a hole in the sole.

Did it hurt when she walked?

Delia felt a tug on her arm and, over the ringing in her ears, she heard Josefita Loma's urgent voice.

"Why are you still here, Delia? Come, they want us in the cafeteria!"

They were alone in the classroom. Some desks had been pushed out of place. Chairs had fallen and open books lay abandoned on the floor.

Delia looked up at Josefita and whined, "I can't go anywhere. I messed my clothes! I'm wet!"

Josefita helped her up. "Let me see . . . Whoa!"

Josefita's eyes widened and she giggled while she slipped off her raincoat and gave it to Delia.

"You had to pick this time to become a *señorita*," she said shaking her head. "Here, put this on. I'll go with you to see the nurse." She helped Delia gather her books.

As they passed the open door to the cafeteria, they heard the school director's angry voice promising a fitting punishment to the ruffian who had thrown the petard in Mrs. Wells' class. The old man's voice became squeaky when he was angry and Delia had seen his face turn tomato red when he became agitated.

He was yelling, "This behavior will not be overlooked! I want names now, or no one will go home today!"

The school nurse was talking on the phone when the girls entered the converted service closet that passed for a clinic near the toilet area.

"Yes, they just left," she said. "They'll be there very soon. You need to know that Mrs. Wells has a heart condition."

The nurse listened for a moment.

"No . . . I don't know about her medication. I'll ask. I'll call you."

After the nurse replaced the receiver on its cradle, Josefita approached her and whispered in her ear.

The nurse looked at Delia and nodded. "I'll take care of it. Thank you. You go on now." She started to usher Josefita out of the clinic.

Josefita stopped briefly and whispered in Delia's ear, "Juan Luis Rubio will be happy to hear it was his petard that made a *señorita* out of Delia Pineda!"

Why couldn't it have been someone else that helped her. Josefita was such a blabbermouth. Soon everyone would know that *la cosa*, "the thing," had come to her.

The nurse reached into a cabinet and pulled out a box of sanitary napkins. "Has your mother talked to you about this, Delia? Do you know what's happened?"

Delia's embarrassment was beginning to turn into anger. Of course Mamá hadn't talked about it; she would wait until it happened, like she had done with María Elena."

"Do you know what to do with this?" the nurse insisted, handing Delia the box.

"Yes. I know. Just let me take care of it and I'll go home," she said, taking the box from the nurse and going into the girls' toilet.

When Delia came out, she still wore Josefita's raincoat. The nurse was on the phone again.

"Yes, *Señora* Pineda. She is fine. I'll send her home in a taxi."

Delia left the box on the nurse's desk. "Thank you," she said, "but I can walk."

On her way home, Delia kept her eyes on the sidewalk. She felt the bulk between her legs. Surely everyone she passed knew that her white school uniform was spotted dark red under Josefita's raincoat. After all, it wasn't even raining anymore.

So this was it. The stinky mess that would come to her every month. Now she was a *señorita*. Now Mamá would see to it that she, just like María Elena, took the recommended doses of Lydia Pinkham's Vegetable Compound, that revolting concoction with its brownish sediment of leaves and God knows what else, and a label with a picture of someone who looked like Queen Victoria. Mamá shook the bottle vigorously to be sure that María Elena, and now Delia, would get everything in the tablespoon, including that vile sediment. The very thought of it made her want to throw up.

"A *señorita*. Big deal! They can have it!" she muttered, and wondered what there was to this that made her older friends and María Elena think they were so special.

She didn't feel special. She felt as if something had been stripped away from her: her childhood. Growing up had been interesting as long as she didn't have to deal with menstruation. Being a *niña* hadn't been so bad, but now that she was an expert at it, the game changed and Delia wondered if she would be up to it. She sensed that she had been marked. As if someone had placed a giant red X over her that said, "Hey, everyone, this is today's *señorita!*"

A mangy cat jumped up from inside a trash can and looked at her. Its meow insulted her. She tried to kick it and missed.

It was nearly midnight when Delia pulled on the new pink nightgown Mamá had given her as a birthday present. She touched the gold, heart-shaped locket hanging from a delicate chain around her neck. Papá had kissed her on both cheeks when he gave it to her at her *quinceañera*.

After all the music, the applause, and the laughter, all that remained were the cacophony of sounds coming from the garden, the nightly serenade from the frogs, the chirping insects, barking dogs, and the voices coming from the kitchen below, where María Elena helped Juliana straighten things up.

Delia finished brushing her hair, held the brush on her lap and studied her reflection in the mirror.

Nothing new. Rites of passage can be imperceptible.

She left the brush on the dresser and picked up the small package that María Elena had left on her bed.

Typical of María Elena, Delia thought, to wait until the last moment to give me a present.

Tied to the package was a pink balloon inscribed *"¡Feliz Cumpleaños!"* She let the balloon float to the ceiling.

"It's time to start filling blank pages," the card said. "Welcome to the club, *Señorita* Delia Susana Pineda!" It was signed, "Your loving sister, Nena."

"Hmm. What one has to go through to be loved!" Delia said, and realized that she had talked to herself more than usual on this day.

She unwrapped the gift to find a locked diary covered in pale blue silk. She unlocked it with the tiny key, riffled the pages and slammed it closed.

A diary called for drama. How would she start?

Dear Diary: Today Mamá told me that I am a young woman now and that I must be careful not to be alone with gentlemen or young boys because they only want one thing from women, and I must save myself for my husband. I wondered if *abuela* said the same thing to her. If she did, what happened? Mamá said that I must tell her every month when I have cramps and she will give me a hot water bottle to put on my belly. To let her know when I run out of Kotex. End of instructions. As for Josefita, she owes me a big one. All those looks and giggles from the girls at my party. And the way Juan Luis Rubio said, *"Señorita* Pineda, I heard your special day started with a bang!" as if it didn't bother him that Mr. Summers suspended him from school for a week and Mrs. Wells will be shipped back to the United States as soon as she gets out of the hospital. María Elena danced with Alberto Guzmán most of the evening . . .

Delia stopped pondering her imaginary entry and laid the diary on her pillow. She reached for the string that dangled from the balloon and, barefoot, walked out the louvered door to the balcony.

She breathed in the aroma of the night blooming jasmine that crept up the patio supports; downstairs, the hammock creaked under Mamá and Papá's weight.

"You seem pensive, *mi vida*," Papá said. "What's bothering you?"

Mamá didn't answer right away. Then, "I don't know, Nacho. It was bad enough to worry about María Elena growing up. Now Delia is *toda una señorita*, too. I dread what's coming: the boys, then the men. If only she had been a boy. It is different, you know, boys don't have babies." Her voice broke and Delia knew Mamá was about to cry.

"No, *mi vida*, don't think that way. María Elena will be all right. And Delia, well, Delia is wiser than you think. And stop being pessimistic. It won't happen to them. They are well chaperoned. Here, wipe off those tears."

Delia heard Mamá blowing her nose.

"Nacho, I just don't seem to be able to get close to Delia. She is still a mystery to me. That tiny premature baby is growing up and is more you than me."

"Everyone is different, *mi vida*. And everyone changes with time. One of these days, Delia will lose her interest in what I do and in my conversations with the Jesuits. Then she'll seek you. She'll be trying to make up for lost time."

"How am I going to guide our daughters, Nacho? How am I going to control them? How am I going to keep them pure?" Mamá said, breathless.

"You don't control them, Berta. They'll stumble a time or two, but with discipline, with love, they'll take the right path. They are good girls, *mi amor*, you are a good mother to them. Just enjoy watching them grow."

"But they need to be watchful of so much they don't know about. If I bring up certain things with them, I may be opening a Pandora's box!"

"Shh, shh," Papá said. "No one will be opening any Pandora's box. Trust the girls to do what is right, *mi amor*."

"I just don't want them to find out about things that could hurt them. I want to protect them, Nacho. I don't ever want to explain to Delia . . ."

"Explain what?"

"Their differences. How could I look her in the eye and admit my sin . . ."

Papá's tone changed. He was firm, no longer placating when he responded.

"We don't protect anyone by keeping things under wraps. I agree that there are matters which we prefer they don't know."

"But what if she asks?"

"We must tell her the truth. María Elena doesn't have unanswered questions. She knows about her birth and it hasn't hurt her."

"But Delia is different, Nacho," Mamá insisted.

"Yes. She's introspective, but she also wants to know the what and why, and she asks questions. I may not answer all her questions, but those I answer, I answer with the truth. So should you, Berta. She can handle it."

"She turns to you, Nacho. She is much closer to you," Mamá said.

"That may be. And that may change some day."

Mamá and Papá fell silent.

Delia leaned against the wall. Her parents' conversation seemed to belong down there, in the hammock only. Up here in the balcony, she was alone in a new space that enveloped her. Beyond that space stood Papá: loving, hard-working, good-natured, trustworthy. Sure of himself. Further away stood Mamá: a seemingly calm beauty who loved her, yes, but who more often than not embraced her older daughter with what Delia perceived as complicity. As if the two of them were bonded by the circumstance of María Elena's birth which made them stand closer together against any intrusion.

Was it the fear of being discovered? Did they think Delia would love them less, or claim Papá solely for herself?

How sad, she thought, that Mamá had chosen to shoulder such a heavy burden, a willing prisoner of her past.

She heard the rattle of the chains that suspended the hammock.

"I'm going to bed, *mi amor*," Papá said, "Come with me?"

Silence. Then the last release of the hammock's chains. They were going inside.

Delia leaned on the balcony railing, gazing beyond the dark silhouette of the treetops. She mentally rehearsed a new initial entry for her diary:

> Dear Diary: *Hoy mi niñez se tiñó de sangre y dejó de ser.* Today, my childhood was tinged with blood and ceased to be.

A tear rolled down her cheek as Delia let go of the balloon and watched it float away into the darkness, until the words *"¡Feliz Cumpleaños!"* had become a part of the night.

Chapter 9

A winter storm pelted the city. Heavy, blackened clouds brought thunder and lightning, and in some areas culverts filled and overflowed. Cars stalled on the streets where the pavement disappeared under muddy torrents. Nothing out of the ordinary for a winter in the tropics. Mother Nature's way of inducing endurance and reminding mortals of who is in control.

A few hardy souls had ventured out, resigned to getting drenched, but Delia chose to stay at the school's library until the downpour ceased. Most of that time, she grappled with an algebra assignment, her hatred for the subject increasing. She knew algebra would be worthless to her in the future because she saw her destiny as a poet, not a mathematician.

She walked home alone, skipping over puddles, staying under the shelter of overhanging balconies and away from the spray from vehicles as they passed her.

Delia ducked quickly into the front door avoiding drips from the overflowing gutters and the clay flower pots brimming with carnations and geraniums on the balcony above. She slipped off her wet brown leather loafers, picked them up and had started up the stairs, when María Elena bumped her before she slammed the door on her way out.

A brief glance at María Elena's swollen nose and red eyes put Delia on guard.

She found Mamá in their bedroom, her back to the entry door. Several drawers in María Elena's dresser were open and in disarray. When the gate slammed and the latch rattled, Mamá leaned out the window and watched María Elena walk away.

Delia dropped her shoes on the floor and Mamá turned and faced her.

Mamá's clenched jaws, the deep furrows between her eyebrows and her tightened fists frightened Delia.

"Where have you been? You are nearly two hours late!"

There was more anger than concern in Mama's voice and she didn't wait for an answer.

"What have you done with my medallion? Your father and I are going out tonight and I plan to wear it. María Elena doesn't have it. Where is it, Delia?"

Mama's medallion, an ancient gold doubloon set in an elaborate gold filigree frame that dangled from a gold box chain, was a link to her family history. Cipriano Hurtado had given it to his bride on their wedding day. Cipriano, born in Acapulco, had answered the call of the sea in his youth when he became a merchant seaman. His work took him to the Isthmus, where he met Rosaura Moreno and fell for the blond, blue-eyed daughter of a customs official. He never returned to Mexico, and Mamá was the fruit of their union. Mamá told Delia once that *Abuelo* Cipriano had found the doubloon while diving off the coast off Acapulco.

Mamá came closer and when she met her eyes, Delia saw in them a mixture of anger and disappointment. Mamá's eyes, for as long as Delia could remember, accused, forgave, loved, and warned with convincing eloquence.

Mamá eyes no longer looked down to meet Delia's. Now her daughter was as tall as Mamá was.

"I am waiting. Where is the medallion?"

"I don't know, Mamá. The last time I saw it you were wearing it."

"Yes. And that was nearly a year ago. At your *quinceañera*. Now I can't find it, and one of you has to know where it is. Juliana doesn't mess with my things. I trust her. María Elena doesn't have it. She already told me she hasn't seen it. So I want to know what you did with it, Delia!"

"I swear to you Mamá, I haven't seen it! Maybe—"

Mamá's hand flew across Delia's cheek and knocked her onto her bed. As she reached to her face, Delia felt tears streaming down from her burning eyes.

"How dare you swear!" Mamá shouted. "Take off your school uniform. I'll be back. You better be ready to tell me where the medallion is or you'll regret it!"

Mamá let the door slam as she left the room.

Delia felt dizzy and sat on the bed for a moment, confused, before she started to unbutton her blouse. Although one of Mamá's sayings was that a child was never too old to be disciplined by a parent, the last time Mamá had hit her, Delia had been twelve years old and the punishment had been shared by María Elena. Delia could not even remember what brought about the punishment.

Downstairs, Mamá yelled at Juliana.

Mamá's irritability had increased in recent months. This woman—for whom the rule was to be soft-spoken, who expressed anger only behind clenched teeth, concerned with what the neighbors would hear and say—seemed to lose control when she dealt with her daughters. More so with Delia than with María Elena. Delia had started to notice the change soon after she had begun to menstruate. Her growing up seemed to annoy her mother. Instead of becoming closer, as had been the case with María Elena, Mamá seemed to resent Delia's maturity.

Would it be different if she had been born a boy and fulfilled her mother's wish to present Papá with a son?

Delia had changed into a short housedress and was standing when Mamá returned with a folded newspaper under her arm and a large wooden bowl full of broken dried corn kernels.

"Now, tell me . . ." Mamá wasn't shouting any more, but the tone of her voice was just as menacing when she planted herself, feet apart, immovable, in front of Delia.

She looked at Delia slowly, from head to toe and back, as if measuring her. Rage seemed to intensify in her widening eyes.

"You won't talk? You won't tell me?" Mamá prodded.

"But I don't know . . . I haven't seen it, please!"

Delia shut her eyes tight to hold back the torrent she knew would come soon. She heard the thud of the wooden bowl full of cracked corn when Mamá set it on the floor and, when she opened her eyes, Mamá was spreading out the newspaper at Delia's feet. She watched her mother pour and spread a thick layer of dried corn kernels on the newspaper. The only other time Mamá had brought out dried corn as punishment was when María Elena had been caught smoking in the girls' toilet at school. Delia remembered how María Elena had cried and screamed when some kernels had cut through the skin on her knees.

Delia held her arms tightly across her chest as if to protect herself for the assault that awaited her.

She pleaded some more, "I really don't know anything about the medallion, Mamá. Please . . ."

Doña Berta Pineda placed her hands on her daughter's shoulders and pushed her down hard.

"Then kneel on the corn. You'll stay there until you are ready to be honest with me."

Sharp kernel fragments dug into Delia's knees and pressed the scant flesh against the bone. She bit her lips hard and watched Mamá turn around and leave the room, quietly closing the door behind her.

Delia began humming to keep from whimpering. She slowly gave in to the pain and took it in as part of her own being.

Penance. But for what: the lost medallion, or for growing up?

More than an hour must have passed when Delia heard the door open again. Her eyes were closed and her chin had dropped against her chest. She had almost dozed off, numbed by the pressure of the broken corn kernels against her knees, but she remained upright, sitting lightly on her heels. Papá walked in and helped her up.

"When you are ready, come down to the *sala*," he said. There was no emotion in his words. Just a dry, tired command, filled with disappointment.

Delia examined herself. The corn had not broken the skin, but her numbed knees tingled as the nerve endings awakened and Delia walked to the bathroom after Papá left the room. She let cool water run on a washcloth and squeezed it just enough so it wouldn't drip. She placed the cloth on one knee for a moment, then on the other. She wasn't bleeding, but the imprint of the corn kernels remained on the swollen, reddened skin, while the agony of her punishment tore at her heart. Some of the kernels had almost cut through. As she walked slowly down the stairs, it hurt each time she bent her knees.

Papá waited in the *sala*. He puffed on a cigarette and leaned an elbow on the radio console, catching the latest news.

When Delia entered, he reached for the cut glass ashtray on top of a table, snuffed out his cigarette and turned off the radio. He placed a hand on Delia's shoulder, searched her eyes.

"Delia, I don't need to remind you that there is a straight line between you and me. You and I don't talk around in circles. *¿Comprendes?*"

She nodded, pressed her lips together and swallowed.

"What do you know of your mother's medallion, *hija?*"

"*Nada*, Papá. I told Mamá. She won't believe me."

Not only had she suffered unjust punishment, but now Papá doubted her and that hurt even more. Delia raised her voice in protest. "María Elena didn't have to kneel on corn. It isn't fair!"

Papá signaled restraint with his hands.

"Don't shout, *hija*. And don't question your mother's discipline. She is very upset. The medallion means a lot to her, you know that."

She started to whimper. "But why am I the only one who—"

The phone rang once, twice, and Papá reached for it.

"Yes? . . . Justo?" He listened, ran his fingers through his hair and frowned. "Oh, no! How did it happen? Where is she? I'll meet you there right away."

Papá hung up and turned to Delia. "Ana's had a stroke. She is in the hospital. She may be dying."

Delia gasped, raised her hands to her chest, and followed Papá as he took his hat off the rack and called out to Mamá.

"Berta! Berta! Come quickly. We have to go to the hospital. Ana's had a stroke!"

"*¡Madre mía!*" Mamá rushed in from the kitchen, untying her apron. She dropped it on a chair, picked up her purse from the top of a bookcase, shouted at Juliana to take charge, and followed Papá out the door.

Delia stood at the front door, her heart beating wildly, and watched them leave in the family's car with Papá at the wheel. He knocked down an empty trash can as he pulled out of the carport.

Delia went back inside, shaking her head.

Ana? A stroke? Dying? She tried to understand and felt a shiver run down her back.

Juliana waited at the kitchen door. Behind her, María Elena stood in the middle of the room, holding some napkins, her mouth open, eyes like saucers.

"What is it, *niña?*" Juliana asked, a look of concern on the sharp planes of her face highlighted by the soft glow from the dying sun that streamed through the patio door.

"It's Isabel's mother. She's had a stroke," Delia said. She couldn't tell them that Ana could be dying. She wouldn't say the words that could make it true.

The old servant crossed herself and opened her arms to the two young women. The three embraced and cried.

"Ave María, llena eres de gracia . . ." Juliana began.

The praise and plea in their sorrowful prayer rose up to the heavens. That may have been the moment when Ana, the laundress without a husband, who bore three children and had a grandson baptized the same day his parents were married, was called to render account to God.

It was early evening two days later, when María Elena and Delia entered the *sala* in Ana's small apartment. In the darkened room, women dressed in black fingered the worn beads of their rosaries and mumbled prayers. Some of them sniffled, or dabbed at their eyes with lacy white handkerchiefs.

All the pictures and the mirror that hung from the walls had been covered with white sheets.

In the center of the room, an open mahogany casket, supported by three black sawhorses, held Ana's body in cushioned white silk like a shell presenting a rare pearl that no one would buy. Four tall silver candlesticks, one at each corner of the casket, held white candles. The flames flickered with the soft breeze that came in through an open window. The smoke and the odor of the burning candles floated in the room like a tenuous blanket of sorrow.

María Elena crossed herself after a cursory look at Ana's face, bowed her head and went to sit next to Mamá.

Delia saw Ana's waxen skin, the color of dark amber, her closed eyes and her thin, pale lips slightly parted. She saw the cotton balls stuffed in Ana's nose. She saw the wrinkled, lifeless hands held as if in prayer, holding a small crucifix. Ana didn't smell of asafetida anymore. Or *Evening in Paris*. The odor of formaldehyde overpowered the bouquet of white lilies that rested on top of the closed half of the casket.

So this wasn't Ana. She had left this body behind in the hospital room the day before, when Isabel had fainted in Justo's arms and Delia had seen two grown men, Tito and Beto, cry like babies.

Ana got her way. She died whole, taking with her all her parts. The aneurysm that caused her headaches, left untreated, had exploded. That's what Papá had said, adding, "At least she went quickly, didn't suffer."

Isabel sat with the other women and stared at her mother's casket, her only motion a slow nodding when someone came to her to express condolences. Sometimes she walked to the center of the room to look at her mother as if expecting her to revive.

One of the women brought Toñito in and handed Isabel a length of blue ribbon. She measured her son, clipped the ribbon, and wrote his name on it with a pen. Then she walked to the casket and placed the ribbon alongside her mother.

"Here he is with you, Mamá, don't come looking for him here," she sobbed as if a claw had grasped her heart and tugged at it.

Doña Berta and two other women helped Isabel back to the straight wooden chair that was her place at her mother's wake.

Across the room, in a corner, Ana's old rocker, where she had rocked her children and her grandchild to sleep, remained empty.

Delia felt tears running down her cheeks. She didn't wipe them off. She tried to focus on the rosary prayer, but she was already missing Ana. She ached for Toñito, whose sun rose and set on his *abuelita*.

A tall, white man arrived at the wake and approached Isabel. His tan linen suit, white shirt, and a loosely tied blue necktie set him apart. Like a stray piece from another puzzle, he didn't fit into the humble crowd that mourned Ana's passing.

When Isabel saw him, she stood up and rushed into his arms, her weeping and sobbing so wrenching, that the man's clean-shaven face contorted with grief.

Delia saw his eyes: a blend of soft green and orange like Isabel's. His hair, graying at the temples, was straight and black like Isabel's also.

The man held Isabel close to him as they both approached Ana's casket. They stood there for a long time, looking at the dead woman and weeping.

Then the man leaned over and kissed Ana's forehead.

Suddenly, as if the man's kiss on her mother's cold face had awakened years of hatred in her, Isabel began punching him with her fists. Hard. Everywhere she could reach him. He tried to hold her arms away and couldn't. Isabel wept and screamed.

"Why now, *hijo de puta*! Where were you when she needed you! Where were you when I was wearing hand-me-downs! Where were you when she had to take in laundry to feed me! *¡Desgraciado! ¡Maldito!*"

The insults poured from Isabel like hot lava along with the physical assault; her long braid came undone and swung free, giving her a crazed look.

Delia wondered if Ana's spirit had possessed the daughter to take revenge before it left this world for good.

The flicker of the candles quickened.

The *rezadoras* cowered, their prayers forgotten.

Delia looked at Mamá. Why didn't she intervene? But Mamá cringed with her arms around María Elena, their eyes full of the same terror that had paralyzed the rest of the women. Now Delia felt it too. She wanted to flee the stifling room, but when she stood up, she had no way to go. The door was blocked. Men bumped into each other when they rushed into the room, took hold of Isabel, and forced her to sit down again.

She tried to shake them off and screamed at the man, "Get out, damn you! Get out! Stay out of my life like you stayed out of hers, you son of a bitch!"

Delia had seen threatened dogs cower, put their tails between their legs and run. This man reminded her of those dogs. He looked around at the men that surrounded him and began to back out of the room, brushing back his tousled hair, he gestured toward Isabel as if pleading, but said nothing.

At the door, Justo grabbed the lapels of the man's suit in his fist and shook him like a rag doll.

"Stay away from her! If you ever come near her again," he said, "I'll kill you!"

Delia knew he meant it. She saw the depth of his fury in his reddened face, the veins that strained to pop on his neck and and his forehead, the dead white of his fists.

Isabel shook and sobbed when Justo took her into the bedroom.

Delia's head felt as if it were about to explode, thumping along with her heart. The whole episode with the stranger had happened in less than two minutes, but it felt as if it had lasted much longer.

She watched Mamá let go of María Elena and follow Justo and Isabel into the bedroom. She heard the murmur of the *rezadoras,* some of them crossing themselves and holding their rosaries to their breasts. María Elena's eyes were fixed to the floor.

Would María Elena react like Isabel in a similar situation? Would she reproach the man who had denied her his name?

Delia stepped outside where the air wasn't as heavy, where things had shape and form, where nothing was blurred.

Before long, the gossip subsided. The sounds that led neighbors and friends to the wake returned: the shuffling of wooden dominoes on tables made of upended crates holding planks of wood. The murmur of the men's voices continued as they emptied bottles of beer and ate from the assortment of casseroles brought in by the women, the smell of food blending with their musk. The squeals of children playing hide-and-seek mixed with the occasional bark of a dog.

Delia stood near the door and watched young men teasing, joking, their voices lowered to a whisper, as they gathered around the older men who slapped down dominoes.

Alberto Guzmán was among those who glanced at the women as they entered the room to join the *rezadoras* praying for the redemption of Ana's soul. Leaning against the wall, he had the look of a stallion straining against the reins. The high humidity matted his hair and polished his face to a glow. The sleeves of his white shirt were rolled up past his elbows.

He was undoing the third and fourth buttons on the front of his shirt, when Delia saw a pendant on his chest catch the light from a street lamp. She began to breathe faster and kept her eyes fixed on him until the light, warm breeze blew open his shirt again and Mamá's doubloon shone.

Late the following night, in their room, Delia confronted her sister.

"I am tired of this, María Elena. I can't go on covering up and taking the punishment for you."

Delia's whisper was more like a whimper. She sat on the edge of María Elena's bed soon after they had turned off the light.

Ana's somber burial under the morning rain was a foggy memory for Delia now. She had waited to talk to María Elena about her discovery.

"I don't know what you are talking about." María Elena rolled over and pulled the sheet up to her chin.

Delia shook her sister's shoulder. "I am talking about you and Alberto Guzmán and Mama's medallion that he is wearing."

María Elena sat up, grasped Delia's arms and dug her fingernails into the bare flesh.

"*¡Maldita metiche!* You've been spying on me! You are jealous!" Her eyes narrowed. "I've seen you looking at Alberto lately. You wish he would take notice of you, huh?"

Delia freed herself from her sister's grasp and her face came closer to María Elena's. "I am not talking about Alberto. I am talking about Mamá's pendant and the punishment *I* took for it. You lied to her and got away with it. She isn't speaking to me. I've had enough! Get the medallion back from him and put it where it belongs with Mamá's things." She begged, "Please, María Elena, get it back!"

"No!" María Elena stood up and walked toward the foot of the bed. "And if you don't shut up about this," she held up her arms, "I'll slash my wrists with one of Papá's razor blades."

"You wouldn't."

"Oh no? You just go ahead and blab about it, you'll see." María Elena got into her bed and leaned back against the headboard. Calmly, as if she had just come out of a relaxing bath, she went on: "Just think about it. It'll be the end of me, but you'll have to live with the pain you cause Mamá, because I'm her first born . . ."

Delia tasted bitter bile and ran out of the room.

After she had flushed her vomit down the toilet, she rinsed her mouth and washed her face with cool water. In the mirror above the sink she saw sadness in her eyes, defeat in the downward curve of her mouth. She looked down.

"Am I protecting Mamá, or am I a coward?"

She gripped the edge of the sink to control her anger. "I don't want to be responsible for anyone's death . . ."

The knot in her bowels loosened. She gathered up her night-gown and sat on the toilet, wrinkling her nose at the putrid smell.

When she returned to the room, her nightgown was soaked with perspiration and her legs felt like lead.

María Elena, Delia knew, was feigning sleep.

She walked to the window, lifted her head up to the night sky and closed her eyes.

"My mother, the mother of my mother . . . Damn them!"

Chapter 10

After Ana's death, Delia noticed, María Elena spent more time at Isabel and Justo's apartment entertaining Toñito. From a distance, she had seen Alberto Guzmán walk with them to the park, her sister next to Alberto.

Since the night when she had confronted María Elena about Mamá's medallion being in Alberto's possession, María Elena had found ways to avoid long conversations with Delia and they never brought up the subject of Alberto Guzmán, but the knowledge of him and his link to María Elena remained between the sisters, an invisible boundary neither of them dared violate for their own different reasons.

On a Saturday two months after Ana's funeral, Delia went to the printing shop to help Justo wrap newly bound yearbooks to be delivered to the Jesuits' preparatory institute for boys. During a break, she shared with Justo *empanadas de carne* and lemonade that Juliana had packed for them that morning.

They sat by the window and waved to Toñito when they saw him walking in the direction of the park with María Elena and Alberto, each holding one of the child's hands.

Delia's eyes followed them, until they turned the corner. Then she looked at Justo as he took a bite of an *empanada*.

"Do you think he loves her?"

Justo swallowed and took a sip of lemonade from a blue enameled porcelain cup.

"I don't know. Only he knows that."

"I think she loves him. I don't know about him," Delia said.

"They are young and there are many degrees of love, *chiquilla*. At their age, for both of them, it takes a lot of courage and guessing. When your time comes, you will know what I am talking about."

Delia thought about it for a short while.

"I understand the guessing part, since it takes a long time to really know somebody, but you said 'courage.' You never mentioned that before. We've talked about passion."

"I remember that." He chuckled.

"When does courage become part of the equation of love, Justo?"

He feigned surprise.

"Did you say 'equation'? Are you starting to love algebra, Delia?"

"Stop changing the subject," Delia pointed at Justo. "You brought it up. Now, tell me: What is so courageous about falling in love? Not like in novels, but in real life. Like in the case of those two?" She inclined her head toward the direction where they had seen María Elena and Alberto with Toñito.

She waited patiently while Justo finished his *empanada* and the lemonade.

"Have you heard the story of the Good Friday treasure?" he asked.

Delia sighed. "We are talking about courage, Justo, not about Holy Week. If you want more help with those books, better talk to me now before the break is up."

"I *am* on the subject of courage," he replied, flattening Delia's nose with his index finger. "Just pay attention, because I'll expect a conclusion from you later. You can take as long as you want to think this one over."

Delia leaned comfortably against the window frame and took another bite of her *empanada*.

Justo looked out to the sunlit street overhung with balconies where the lacy patterns of wrought iron festooned brick and masonry buildings brimming with flowers. The shadows of the balcony railings painted intricate designs on the pavement, changing with the time of the day.

Young men had started to gather at the corner, some leaning against the wall outside the neighborhood grocery store, others standing across from them, at the curb, forming a gauntlet for the next shapely woman.

Justo looked at Delia, again ready to meet her challenge.

"Some men claim to have experienced what I'm about to tell you. I haven't, because I have not been chosen. Actually," Justo said, rubbing his chin and frowning, "I hope I'm never chosen."

"Get on with it, Justo." Delia pointed at her watch. "Time's running out!"

"As the story goes, it's been said that avaricious people don't trust banks to keep their money safe. So they bury their money and their jewels."

"So I've heard."

"After they die, their souls linger in limbo, unable to move on to a permanent destination in the hereafter, until they pass their worldly riches, left behind in the burials, to a living soul. This they can only do at midnight, on Good Friday. They choose an heir."

"How?"

"I've no idea, but on Good Friday this heir sees a red flashing light in the distance and approaches it."

Justo moved his arm to indicate a space beyond them and extended his neck as if peering at something.

He's enjoying this, Delia thought. Just like he does when he reads stories to Toñito.

"This isn't from one of Toñito's storybooks, is it?"

"Shh." Justo put a finger to his lips, then his hand moved forward, fluttering toward the distance. "The light moves and he follows it. Then the light stops moving."

Justo stilled his hand, the palm facing away from him. "The light starts to scintillate . . ." He flexed his fingers several times. "Over a certain spot on the ground."

He paused and looked at Delia.

"And?"

He poured more lemonade and took another sip as if preparing for the scene to follow.

"As the heir gets closer, the light starts pulsing bright red, very fast."

The pitch and tone of his voice changed to enliven his narration.

"He hears a thundering herd coming closer, and closer. The rumble, and the trembling of the earth as the hooves pound the ground, overwhelm the heir. The wind blows with hurricane force and there's the wailing and moaning of a thousand voices of the damned surrounding the heir and the light."

Justo paused and took a quick sip of lemonade, without looking at Delia.

"If the chosen heir's ambition overcomes his terror and he digs up the treasure, he inherits the wealth. He also inherits the curse of avarice. If, on the other hand, he flies on the wings of terror, or because his good conscience prevails over his greed, he may remain a poor man who will always have to earn his keep, but he will be free of demons."

Justo smiled and snapped his fingers in front of Delia's face.

Her eyes felt dry. She blinked, shuddered and realized that the rest of her *empanada* was now nothing more than a mass of crumbs in her tightened fist. She wiped her trembling hands on an ink-stained rag.

Justo slapped his thighs and stood up.

"Now, back to work, *chiquilla*. When you have figured it out, tell me where lies the courage. Love, you see, is just as much of a challenge."

Later that afternoon, Delia walked home absorbed in her thoughts and almost bumped into Josefita Loma.

"Look up around you, *niña*, you seem to be counting the bricks on the sidewalk!" Josefita teased. "I have something for you from Juan Luis Rubio. He handed it to me when we left school yesterday. He said, 'Thanks for the loan.'"

Delia smiled as she took a book from Josefita. It was her copy of Federico García Lorca's play *Blood Wedding*.

She had started to read García Lorca's work in books borrowed from the library. Mamá had disapproved. "That man's writing is too revolutionary," she had said, but Papá stood by Delia again.

"The man is a genius, *mi amor*. He may reveal too much of human nature and of his own political philosophy . . . But let Delia read what she wants. I assure you, it won't corrupt her, it'll enrich her."

When Papá said that one day at the breakfast table, María Elena raised her eyebrows at Delia and smirked. Delia raised a finger to her chest, made circles where a medallion would be, and raised her own eyebrows.

Josefita walked along with Delia. "I thought you didn't loan your books. I see Juan Luis must be special," she said, elbowing Delia.

"I just trust him to take care of them. That's all. He returns them promptly, unlike you."

Near the Pinedas' house, a street vendor pushed a cart piled high with fresh coconuts.

"Please carry these, Josefita, Mamá asked me to buy some coconuts today," Delia said, handing her friend an empty Thermos bottle and the book. Then she pulled out a small change purse from her dress pocket and bought two coconuts.

Josefita unlatched the front gate for them. In the kitchen Juliana peeled and chopped *yuca* and *ñame* for a vegetable stew, while Mamá cleaned the silk off the corn to be cooked in its husk over coals on the barbecue pit outside. The smell of marinating meat for *adobo* permeated the room.

Delia lifted the coconuts to the kitchen table.

"Here are the coconuts, Mamá. I'll go upstairs and freshen up. I'm tired, but all the books have been packed. Papá said he'll be home soon."

Two months had passed since the episode of the missing medallion and Mamá was talking to Delia again, but if she had forgiven her daughter she kept that to herself. Delia knew parents didn't ask for forgiveness, or say "I forgive you," and Mamá was not one to break with tradition, even if that meant healing and closing the emotional chasm between them. If a crime of passion was a matter of a man's honor, as Papá had once said, for Mamá, expressing forgiveness verbally would undermine her authority.

"We'll be having dinner on the patio, today," Mamá said. "This is too nice a summer day to waste inside. Are you staying, Fita?"

"No, *Doña* Berta, thank you. I'll just go up with Delia for a while," Josefita said, placing an arm around Delia's shoulder.

Upstairs, Delia started running a bath in the tub. She threw in a little muslin bag with rosemary, jasmine and rose petals to scent the water. When she returned to her room, she saw Josefita sitting at her desk, holding the book in one hand. In the other, she held a white sealed envelope with Delia's name carefully written in Old English script.

Josefita handed the envelope to Delia and stood beside her.

Delia turned the envelope looking for the sender's name.

"It was inside the book," Josefita said.

Delia held the envelope against the light, tore off one end and pulled out a single folded sheet of paper and a strip of finely woven white straw about half an inch wide and five inches long on which her name appeared in black letters. At each end, a very narrow, delicate braid of the same white straw, was tied together to form a bracelet.

Josefita took the woven strip from Delia's hand and let out a loud whistle.

"Somebody has gone to a lot of work to impress you. I know he likes you, but a bracelet, that has meaning!"

Delia placed the folded note inside the book.

"Isn't someone waiting for you at home, Fita?" she said, taking the bracelet from Josefita and placing it on her desk.

She ushered a reluctant Josefita out of the room and out of the house by way of the front door to avoid seeing Mamá.

After she unlatched the front gate for Josefita, Delia hugged her and whispered, "You know, Fita, you are so charming when you are silent. That's when I like you the most."

"You don't need to flatter me, Delia. You can trust me. I won't tell."

"Like you didn't tell anyone the day I became a *señorita*?"

"That was a long time ago. I said I was sorry. Besides, I am older now, with secrets of my own I might reveal to you one day," she teased.

In her room, Delia turned García Lorca's *Blood Wedding* upside down and caught the note as it fell. She unfolded it and began to read.

Dearest Delia,

I admire you deeply. I think of you constantly when I am not near you, and I can't take my eyes from you when you are near me. No one else fills my dreams like you do. No other eyes inflame me like yours do. I tried to match the poets to tell you how I feel, but I can't find the words to describe it. I only know it is LOVE. So I made something for you with my own hands, and in making it, I caressed your face. Before I placed my gift in the envelope, my love, I kissed it, so when you put it on, you'll put on my love and my kiss. That will have to do until the day when my lips can touch yours.

> "Junta tu roja boca con la mía,
> o Estrella la gitana!
> Bajo el oro solar del mediodía
> morderé la Manzana!"

Yours forever,
Juan Luis Rubio

His signature filled nearly a fourth of the page. It didn't surprise Delia. Juan Luis Rubio was charming, but cocky. She read into the absence of paragraphs in the letter, taking that as the outpouring of his emotion, just as the poet had poured his longing in the verse that Juan Luis had carefully copied in elaborate script. She read the poem again:

> *Join your red mouth to mine,*
> *oh gypsy Star!*
> *Under the gold of the noonday sun*
> *I'll bite the apple!*

A hot wave passed through Delia from her feet to her face as she read her first love letter again. She felt blood pulsing throughout her body, pounding at her temples. Her chest tightened, her insides knotted and her face felt flushed. Her skin tingled, as if a thousand hands caressed her. Her nipples hardened and, between her legs, her clitoris began to swell.

She closed her eyes, overwhelmed and frightened by these sensations. She had felt them before when she read some of the books Mamá had blacklisted; but this time the feelings were triggered by a letter from someone real. Someone she knew. Someone with whom she shared part of her days at school, who was part of her crowd of friends.

She conjured Juan Luis Rubio's dark, laughing eyes under bushy brows, his ready smile bracketed by dimples, his unruly wavy black hair, the way he walked as if ready to sprint at a moment's notice and, trembling, she pressed the letter to her lips.

María Elena's footsteps coming into the room brought Delia out of her reverie, but not quickly enough. With shaking hands, Delia slipped the note back in the book.

María Elena approached the desk and picked up the straw bracelet. She turned it this way and that. She even brought it to her nose and smelled it as if its scent would reveal its origin.

"Explain this. I know you didn't make it." María Elena said, shaking the bracelet in front of Delia.

Her harsh tone angered Delia.

"I don't have to explain anything to you, just like you don't have to explain to me your walks with Alberto Guzmán!"

"We'll see about that! As for what goes on between Alberto and me, you know what will happen if you accuse me. So you'll do well to keep your mouth shut!" María Elena threw back the bracelet.

The look in her sister's hazel eyes reminded Delia of an angry cat.

Outside, Juliana shouted from the bathroom, "Who left the water running in the tub? It is about to overflow!"

Delia tossed the bracelet in a desk drawer, grabbed her blue terrycloth robe from a hook behind the door and rushed out of the room. She didn't soak for very long. She knew María Elena would not wait to bring up the subject of the bracelet with Mamá.

Papá must have noticed the tension between his daughters during the dinner hour. He looked from one to the other and made it a point to make superfluous talk while the family ate, keeping the tone light.

Later that evening, when Delia was outside watering Mamá's garden, Papá approached her.

"I am going for a walk on the beach, *querida*," he said. "Your Mamá is expecting Otilia's visit this evening. Want to keep an old man company?"

Delia turned off the hose and Papá helped her coil it next to the wall, then held the gate open for her.

They continued down the narrow sidewalk in silence, Papá lighting a cigarette, Delia pulling off a lavender rose from the climbing bush that overhung their neighbor's wall. She brought it up and smelled the scent of clove. She tore off some leaves and stuck the rose in the braid on the back of her head.

In the distance, the sun sent up its last rays as it dipped into the horizon, painting the sky a bright orange that slowly changed to rose, then glowed in deep watermelon red before it turned to crimson and faded into slate gray. Twilight began to put away the day and the tree frogs and crickets began to serenade the coming night. A gentle breeze carried the scent of carnations and lemon blossoms beyond garden walls. Once the commute time passed, the wide avenue in the city's suburbs was almost empty.

Delia was grateful for her father's patience. He never pressed her for confidences, but he allowed every opportunity. Like now.

"Papá, I got a letter today," she ventured. "It's from Juan Luis Rubio."

"What about?"

"He says he loves me."

Papá put his arm around Delia. "Well, congratulations, *querida*! I knew there would be competition for me soon."

After a few steps, Papá's pride turned to concern. "Is the letter respectful?"

"I think so, Papá."

"You know I will have to speak to him about approaching you that way, *hija*. How do you feel about it?"

"Well, I . . ." What could she say? I felt sexually excited when I read it? No, that wasn't what Papá meant. "I've known him a long time, Papá. His parents are your friends!"

"I mean, what do you think of him as a young man, not as a boy, Delia. It's different. Does he treat his friends with respect? Does he strut around? I know sometimes he joins the boys at the corner and watches the girls go by. Has he followed you with *piropos*?"

Delia felt insulted. "No! No one has, Papá. You know I would not put up with it. I don't give them the chance! That's humiliating!"

"A lot of girls don't think so," Papá tested her.

Delia stopped and faced her father and said firmly, "I am not like 'a lot of girls.'"

Papá smiled. She had passed the test.

"I like him as a friend. He's nice," she said, continuing to walk. "He does well in school. That thing with Mrs. Wells and the firecracker . . . Well, none of us liked her. Juan Luis likes to have a good time, but he is not a bully. He is not vulgar, Papá."

Was she pleading Juan Luis Rubio's case too strongly?

When they reached the beach, they sat on a concrete bench facing the ocean. The full moon had risen and painted a brushstroke of shimmering silver on the water. Delia imagined it was an invitation beckoning her to embark on an unknown voyage where her future could be linked to Juan Luis Rubio. She liked the idea. She liked him.

She watched the white crest of waves at low tide gently lap the sand with a soothing motion. It felt good to talk to Papá about the love letter, but she could not tell him how reading it had stirred in her a yearning she knew would grow with time, like the ocean tide. Slowly growing stronger, swallowing the beach.

"Juan Luis made a woven straw bracelet with my name on it. I would like to keep it, Papá."

"Did he give it to you?" Papá asked while the two of them continued to look ahead toward the distant dark horizon.

"It was with the letter."

"Hm . . . What about the letter, Delia. Do you want to keep that too?"

She turned to him. "May I, Papá? It is the first one."

He smiled at her and nodded. "Yes, *querida*. And hang on to it. You won't be getting another one soon if I have anything to do with it." He placed an arm around her shoulder. "Thank you for telling me. Does Mamá know?"

"She probably knows by now. Nena saw the bracelet but she doesn't know where it came from."

"We can't keep this from Mamá. I'll talk to her. And to Juan Luis Rubio."

Don Nacho took Delia's hand and helped her up from the bench. Then he put both hands on her shoulders and was very serious when he spoke. He didn't raise his voice, but the care with which he enunciated every word impressed in Delia the importance of their meaning. Once in a while he would increase the pressure of his hands on her shoulders slightly for emphasis.

"Delia, *hija*, remember that you are growing older, but you have much of life ahead of you. You will be faced with serious decisions soon enough. Take your time, *hija*. Be responsible. Think things over and always remember that what others think of us, depends on how they see us act. You owe yourself respect. You owe your family respect. I don't want to hear that neighbors are talking about my daughters as if they were tramps. It is your responsibility to keep the family name clean. Watch your behavior. Watch whose company you choose. Observe propriety at all times, *hija*. Don't expect others to do it for you."

Don Nacho Pineda paused and looked deeply into his daughter's eyes for a moment.

"I am understanding to a point, Delia. But it is your responsibility not to make mistakes. *El que corta su palo, que lo cargue. ¿Comprendes?*"

Delia nodded. Yes, she understood one of Papá's favorite sayings: He that chops down his tree has to carry it.

Today she had crossed a threshold further into adulthood. She sensed that this talk should have come from Mamá.

It occurred to her that, had she been born a boy, Papá may have encouraged his son to be a *macho*, to taste as much forbidden fruit as he could, but to be sure of the purity of the woman to whom he gave his name. But being a girl, she would be held responsible for her family's dignity, for her reputation; so it was up to her to remain untouched, a virgin.

As they strolled back home, Delia remembered Justo's story about the Good Friday treasure and wondered how much courage it had taken for Papá to thumb his nose at convention and ignore *malas lenguas* when he had chosen Mamá to be his life's companion.

Would Juan Luis Rubio be capable of love such as that?

Chapter 11

The day after she received her first love letter, Delia found it difficult to focus her attention during swimming practice. Her mind kept going back to Juan Luis Rubio. She didn't hold up well during the relay and, when she wasn't in the water, she repeatedly glanced at her bare wrist and imagined what it would look like with the straw bracelet wrapped around it. It would show everyone that she was loved. It would mark her as part of a duo. It would tell the world it wasn't Delia Pineda only, but Delia Pineda-and-Juan Luis Rubio, all in one phrase, all together in the exhalation of one single breath.

Papá didn't waste any time. Delia found that out when Juan Luis Rubio met her as she walked home from school.

"*Hola*, Delia," he said, catching up with her and adjusting his long stride to match hers.

The sound of his voice quickened her heartbeat and she answered his greeting with a whispered "*Qué hay*, Juan Luis." She hesitated to say more. Would it be proper to acknowledge the letter and the bracelet by thanking him? She decided against it and let him be the one to bring it up.

"Your father phoned my parents early this morning and invited us to after-dinner coffee at your house tonight," he said. "Do you have any idea why?"

He had stepped in front of her and when she looked at his face, Juan Luis opened his eyes wide in mock wonder, raised and lowered his eyebrows, extended out his arms and his open palms were those of a clown pleading for an explanation.

Delia couldn't keep from laughing and was surprised by how rapidly things had changed for her. Yesterday, before Josefita Loma played courier, Delia could have walked with Juan Luis Rubio and not felt anything out of the ordinary. Then, he was just one of her schoolmates, a friend she had known since they were in grade school together. But now Juan Luis Rubio's presence involved a much different perspective. He had gone beyond mere friendship when he declared his love to her.

She felt that the emotional and physical upheaval that his declaration elicited within her was coming to the surface. That he could sense, smell, hear, and if he looked in her eyes, see the fervor of her response to his letter.

They resumed their walk.

"It is about my letter to you, isn't it, Delia?" he prompted. "Did your parents see it?"

She stopped and faced him.

"No! I didn't show it to them. But you sent a gift with it and María Elena saw that. I couldn't keep secret where the bracelet came from, but I didn't tell her. I told Papá, because he understands. He didn't ask to see anything, but he doesn't want you to send me any more letters. He said he would talk to you about it."

It was a rapid torrent of words—to explain what? That his feelings for her were out in the open?

She restrained herself somewhat. "Papá is right, Juan Luis, we are too young . . ."

Juan Luis touched her arm slightly.

"We won't be too young forever, Delia. This is only the beginning. I may stay away out of respect for you and your parents. But I won't give you up." He paused, then added a firm, "Ever!"

She could still feel the warmth of his fingertips after he took his hand away.

She believed him. Juan Luis Rubio didn't insist that she acknowledge her own feelings for him. Maybe he didn't need to ask. Maybe he saw the answer in the way she laughed at his jokes and conspired with others to cover up his mischievous deeds, like the time he had tossed the firecracker in Mrs. Wells' class. Delia never told Josefita that it was Juan Luis who had put a cricket in her thick curly hair that nearly drove her mad when the insect became entangled, causing her to run home screaming.

And maybe Juan Luis knew that Delia liked him because she had not slapped him for sending her the letter. There had been no outraged "How dare you!" from her.

I may be confused, but I would be lying if I acted offended, she thought.

93

They walked for a short distance in silence, and when they reached the corner where they would turn in different directions toward their own homes, they paused and faced each other.

"I'll see you tonight, Delia. I doubt that I will say much. I have said enough already."

His voice sounded deeper than usual, with a resonance that played inside her and she knew that he meant every word in his letter.

"I'll see you tonight, Juan Luis. I won't say much either." She threw caution to the wind. "Thank you for the letter and for the bracelet. You understand why I can't wear it . . . yet. Don't you?"

He nodded, smiled, clicked his heels together, and brought his fingers to his forehead in a snappy military salute.

"Whatever you say, *señorita* Pineda. *¡Hasta luego!*"

Delia laughed. "*¡Hasta luego*, Juan Luis!" and watched him walk away whistling.

Francisco and Chabela Rubio arrived at the Pineda home with their son about an hour after the Pinedas had finished their evening meal.

Papá had announced their visit earlier, as if no one else knew about it; but in fact, María Elena had been cross with Delia that afternoon and Mamá's kiss when Delia left for school in the morning felt cold.

Delia wondered if Papá had asked her mother to leave to him any discussion related to Juan Luis Rubio.

Juliana had prepared a cashew cake and had set out a bottle of sherry for the adults. She brewed freshly picked peppermint leaves for tea to be served to Juan Luis and the Pineda daughters.

Juliana seemed excited about the Rubio's visit. She sneaked a wink at Delia when they were folding the napkins.

So, Mamá hadn't kept it to herself after all. She had told Juliana. Had Mamá bragged about someone being interested in one of her daughters? No, more likely Mamá felt disturbed, resentful that now she would have to keep a close eye on Delia to make sure she stayed away from the boy, *que no fuera a meter la pata* like Isabel had done. Like Mamá herself had done. Did Mamá ever admit that even to herself?

94

Don Nacho and *Doña* Berta had been waiting in the *sala* and Delia heard them welcome the Rubios at the front door. They were old friends. Francisco Rubio and *Don* Nacho had been school chums and kept up their friendship throughout all the years since. *Don* Francisco owned a Ford automobile agency and Papá had always bought his cars from him.

Juan Luis had inherited his amiable ways from his father, the smile and dimples that welcomed customers and kept the business booming.

Doña Chabela's Italian ancestry came through in her effusive manner, the generous roundness of her body. From her, Juan Luis had inherited the shiny black hair, dark eyes full of mischief, and a belly-laugh that turned heads envious of its gusto.

Juan Luis was the progeny of two strong Latin types and Delia saw this as a mark in his favor. He might be playful, but when it came to his feelings, Juan Luis wasn't namby-pamby. When it came to approaching Delia, he had shown decisiveness.

A serving table had already been set in the *sala*. María Elena and Delia helped Juliana bring in the cake and drinks and Juliana exchanged pleasantries briefly with the Rubios before she retired to the kitchen.

Doña Berta served the cake while *Don* Nacho poured the Jerez. María Elena served the tea.

The adults took over the conversation. They talked about the recent heat wave, the new models Ford was sending to *Don* Francisco's agency the following month and the rumors of a possible *coup d'état* by factions unhappy with the current government.

The Pineda daughters and Juan Luis sipped tea and ate cake. They watched their parents agree, debate in good humor, venture predictions, while the real purpose for the visit seemed suspended above them in the room, like a leaf drifting down slowly, waiting for someone to hold out a hand where it could make contact.

Delia tried to appease the butterflies in her stomach and tried to concentrate on the conversation.

"I'm afraid that those know-it-all kids at the university are going to run to the streets one day soon," *Don* Francisco was saying.

"What's bothering them now?" *Don* Nacho asked, as if the matter had any relevance at the moment.

Delia wished she could reach his leg and kick it, tell him to stop stalling, get on with the reason for the meeting.

"They're talking again about claiming the American military bases in the Canal Zone," *Don* Francisco said.

"That's easier said than done," Papá dismissed the validity of the protesters' quest with a hand gesture.

"It's just the same group of perennial students funded by the communists, Nacho, but they know how to bring up real patriotism to inflame the other students. So even if the coup doesn't happen, we'll have the so-called *universitarios* to contend with."

"That's not good for business," Papá said. "The last time the students ran to the streets, I had to close the print shop for two days. I boarded the front door and the window. I see no need to risk their storming in and toppling shelves stacked with cans of printing ink and tearing down the place. They don't care whether you are for them or against them. Their purpose is to create mayhem."

"I had cars damaged in my lot. They threw rocks and bottles, broke windshields and windows, and dented cars. It cost me a lot to have the cars repaired just so I could sell them, even at a loss." *Don* Francisco shook his head and pressed his lips together, before he lifted his snifter of Jerez and inhaled the sweet liquor.

"Juliana and I had to deal with two of the *universitarios* that jumped over the gate and hid in the bushes from the mounted police," Mamá said. "One had a head wound. He claimed a policeman caused it. But I still think it came from something one of his friends threw."

During a lull in the conversation, *Doña* Chabela asked, "How do you like the nuns at La Santísima Concepción, María Elena?"

Delia watched her sister assume a straighter posture, and extend her little finger when she took a sip of tea, before she answered.

"It's wonderful, *Doña* Chabela."

María Elena took another sip of tea, before she placed the cup and saucer on the side table. She had been drawn into the adult's conversation and María Elena knew how to take advantage of a situation.

"The nuns are very strict, but when we finish our education with them, we are well groomed to move in society. A young lady knows all about propriety and acceptable behavior. We know how to command respect, especially from gentlemen . . ." María Elena boasted.

Delia's eyes sent a message to *Don* Nacho: I don't have to sit here and listen to that, Papá, please?

He immediately responded.

"Yes, that's true, Nena. And that reminds me that you still have homework to do. I think *Don* Francisco and *Doña* Chabela will understand if you say good night now," Papá said.

María Elena stood up, said good night to Juan Luis Rubio's parents, ignored Juan Luis and lifted her chin higher as she walked past Delia.

Juan Luis sent Delia a knowing look. He didn't smile, but his dimples appeared and she knew he was amused by María Elena's remarks.

Had he seen Alberto Guzmán and María Elena together? I hope not, Delia thought.

Papá cleared his throat, a sign he was ready to deal with the reason the two families had come together on short notice.

"Francisco, Chabela, we've known each other a very long time. There's great deal of mutual respect. We've seen our children growing up," Papá looked at *Don* Francisco for agreement.

"Yes, Nacho," *Don* Francisco said. He smiled and held *Doña* Chabela's hand. They shared a sofa separated from Juan Luis' chair by a side table.

The serving table and the empty chair where María Elena had sat separated Delia from Juan Luis Rubio.

Papá took a sip of Jerez. Delia felt the cake she had eaten creeping back up and she sipped tea to keep her nerves under control. Things were moving slowly, with Papá introducing the subject as if he were approaching a congested intersection, wary not to rear-end someone. In this case, Papá respected the long friendship and would not risk even a single word that might insult the Rubios.

"Francisco, your Juan Luis has approached our Delia with a love letter and a small gift that he made. It seems he thinks that he loves her. I'm sure you'll understand that the two of them are still too young to be involved as *enamorados*. Berta and I" —he looked at Mamá and she nodded agreement— "would like to ask Juan Luis . . ."

Papá looked at Juan Luis, and the young man's eyes held *Don* Nacho's.

". . . would like to ask Juan Luis now, with the two of you present, that he refrain from writing that sort of letter to Delia, it doesn't seem proper at this time."

Papá looked at Delia and she, too, held his look. How could he deny her the thrill of receiving more love letters? She had agreed to it, but couldn't he ease up a bit?

Mamá rushed her own opinion. "Delia is only a child, Chabela, she isn't sixteen yet!"

"She'll be sixteen next month, *mi amor*," Papá said, patting the hand where Mamá clenched a folded napkin. "Not that it makes a difference, because she needs to complete her high school education and I know that she plans to continue further. Having a *novio* at this stage is out of the question. It would be a distraction and we want her to put all her attention in her studies," Papá addressed *Don* Francisco directly.

Don Francisco turned to his son and nodded.

Delia wasn't surprised when Juan Luis addressed her father, his voice calm, serious. At that moment sixteen-year-old Juan Luis Rubio had the self-assurance of an older man.

"*Don* Ignacio, with all respect to you and *Doña* Berta, and with all respect to my parents, I'll answer you. I promise you that I won't approach Delia again with letters. But what I feel for your daughter is sincere and pure. Because of that, I won't do anything to blemish her reputation, *Don* Ignacio, you can be sure of that. But when the time comes, I will ask my parents to speak with you and ask for your permission so that I can visit Delia as her *novio* . . ."

Juan Luis Rubio turned to look at Delia.

Their eyes met just long enough for her to feel the warmth that rose up from her chest and tingled her cheeks. She wanted to smile at him, to let him know that she was the one who counted. But not with everyone watching.

". . . if she feels the same way about me. Until that time, *Don* Ignacio, I ask that you allow me to continue to be her friend."

"Nacho," *Don* Francisco said, "you know that I've raised my son to be honorable. If you allow your daughter to continue her friendship with him, I give you my word, as he gives you his, that he will respect her."

"It isn't my intention to end a friendship, Francisco. As far as Berta and I are concerned, there is no objection to their friendship, as long as they are with others, their own families, their friends. But we don't want to give reason for gossip." Papá's voice had a tone of relief. These were things that needed to be said, established.

Papá's eyes met Delia's. She remained still, her hands folded in her lap. She could feel Mamá's eyes on her, also.

Delia knew that she was not expected to take part in this conversation. It was about her, yes, but it was to be decided by men. Even *Doña* Chabela had kept quiet and Mamá's opinion really hadn't meant much.

At that moment, Delia resented them all. Even Juan Luis, whose promise was taken into consideration. Her own feelings weren't. Not at this time when the rules were being set. The cards were held by Papá, *Don* Francisco, and Juan Luis. The men decided the game plan. Otilia was right. Women's lives bore the thumbprint of one man or another.

Don Francisco spoke again. "It's clear then. We are in agreement." He stood up and Juan Luis followed his father's lead. Papá stood up also. The two older men shook hands and embraced each other.

"*Amigos*, Nacho, *siempre amigos*," *Don* Francisco said.

Papá and Juan Luis shook hands. Mamá and *Doña* Chabela embraced each other.

It was then that *Don* Francisco came to Delia, took her hands gently in his and helped her stand up. He hugged her as he always did, since she was a little girl. Then he turned to his son and gestured, as if presenting her.

"This is a precious jewel, Juan Luis, always treat her as one or you'll respond to me."

Juan Luis' eyes were moist. He shook his father's hand. Delia knew he was making his father a promise and, in doing so, he was promising to her, also. Someday, he would hold her and whisper that promise without witnesses.

"Well, it's getting late," *Don* Francisco said. He put an arm over *Doña* Chabela's shoulders and the other over Mamá's. "We must be going . . ."

They all walked out to the front gate and after their good nights, the Pinedas waited until the Rubios' car was almost out of sight before going back into the house.

A light drizzle began spotting the walkway.

It's going to rain tonight, Delia thought. Once, Ana had told her that if it rained when big events took place in your life, it meant that the event had God's blessing. She turned her face to the night sky and let the fine drizzle wet it.

Inside, Papá turned on the radio and searched the dial for the evening news.

Without speaking to Delia, Mamá began to stack the empty dishes and glasses and took them into the kitchen. Delia followed her with the leftover cake and the empty bottle of Jerez.

"Go up to bed, Delia. It's late. Good night," Mamá said, brushing her daughter's cheek with a soft kiss, but Delia sensed there was more habit than feeling in the kiss.

María Elena leaned against the kitchen counter, her arms crossed over her chest, staring at Delia.

Delia felt a battle brewing and opted for a retreat. She went back to the *sala*.

"Good night, Papá." She kissed his cheek. "And thank you," she whispered.

Don Nacho gave her a stern look. But she could detect laughter behind it.

"Good night, *querida*. And behave yourself!"

Later, when Delia heard María Elena enter the room, she pretended sleep. She knew she would hear from Mamá tomorrow and she didn't want to deal with María Elena now.

Chapter 12

Mamá, as Delia had suspected she might, took things a bit further. She assigned María Elena to watch over Delia and report any unbecoming conduct by her youngest daughter. The news of Delia's first love letter had upset *Doña* Berta. A sixteen-year-old girl who received such correspondence was a *sinverguenza* in Mama's eyes.

She stood in the girls' bedroom with her arms akimbo.

"You must have encouraged him. Just stop to think about this! It is something your older sister has never done! At your age, acting like a tramp! Why can't you learn from Nena's example! She is a decent girl," Mamá said, her face becoming more livid.

Why should being loved by someone make a woman a tramp? Wasn't Mamá loved by Papá? Did that make her a tramp? Mamá's contradictions made less sense each time they surfaced. Was Mamá afraid that her daughters would turn up one day with bastard children? Or was she afraid they would not, and then the magnitude of her own sin would multiply? Would Mamá ever find it in her soul to forgive herself? All these thoughts bounced around in Delia's head. She saw Mamá's lips move, but she wasn't listening.

María Elena, standing behind Mamá and leaning on the door frame, tsk, tsked shaking her head, mocking Delia.

"Stop it, María Elena!" Furious, Delia turned to her mother. "She's no saint, Mamá, she—"

Delia didn't finish. Mama's lips tightened, she raised her chin, and her look warned Delia to keep her mouth shut or things would get worse.

Behind Mamá, María Elena turned and left the room.

Still frowning, Mamá came closer to Delia, placed her hands on her daughter's shoulders and shook her gently.

"Don't involve Nena in your reprehensible behavior. Your older sister has never given us these problems. She's a decent *señorita* and I won't allow you to put blame on her." Her voice softened. "Now, promise me, *hija*, that you'll do as I say. I don't want to see you disgraced. *Me matarías si metes la pata.*"

Mamá looked so frightened, so desperate, it broke Delia's heart.

"I will Mamá. You know I'll listen to you. I won't 'put my foot in it.'"

No, Mamá, I won't get pregnant unless I have a husband. You can be sure of that. Delia promised silently.

When Mamá left the room, Delia sat on her bed and looked for a long time at the book that rested on her desk and held between its pages Juan Luis Rubio's letter. She understood why Mamá was so upset. Delia had reached the age when Mamá would have to explain to her *cosas de gente grande*. Would Mamá ever be able to share secrets with her? Would Mamá ever love her with the same blinding devotion as she loved her bastard daughter? Would Mamá ever protect her the way she shielded María Elena from everyone? Would Mamá ever forgive her for endangering her life at the moment of her premature birth, when eclampsia attacks had almost killed them both? Was it then that the seed of rejection was planted in Mamá's heart?

Delia remembered the day when Brother Cristóbal had stopped at the printshop and she was helping Justo count pages to be stacked on the printing machines. Chatting with Papá, the Jesuit had remarked on the closeness between father and daughter.

"She is very precious to me," Papá had said. "Did you know that we didn't name her until she was two weeks old?"

Brother Cristóbal sunk his hands in the pockets of his soutane.

"Why, Nacho? Didn't you have any names in mind?"

"Oh, yes, we had names. But when we took Berta to the hospital in the ambulance, the convulsions were so severe, she was foaming at the mouth and her eyes were rolled back. Doctor Cabrillo said I had to make a choice: the mother or the child. With my heart tearing in pieces, I chose the mother. But God is so merciful, Brother. He gave me both!"

Brother Cristóbal made the sign of the cross between them.

"She was so tiny, that I could hold her in the palm of my hand. She wasn't expected to live. There wasn't an incubator available and the nurses kept her cuddled in warm cotton pads."

Papá looked at Delia while he told Father Cristóbal the story.

"They dabbed olive oil on her to keep her skin from drying out. For seven days I prayed to every saint. I called on my mother's soul to save her." Tears had welled in his eyes.

Delia knew then that Mamá had not forgiven her the suffering that preceded her birth. She supposed that now Mamá had another resentment to pile up on the stack.

Delia was getting the attention of young men, and that, if you asked Mamá, led only to corruption and unmentionable doings.

The way Mamá bristled at conversation that approached the subject of sex, brought Delia to conclude that, if it depended on Mamá, the human race would come to a sudden end. After all, lacking a male offspring, Papá's line was already doomed to extinction.

That evening, in the *sala*, Delia read from her history textbook while Mamá and Papá played cards quietly. Delia felt uncomfortable in the tense atmosphere underlined by the unusual lack of music in the room. Delia sensed that the conversation of the night before with the Rubios, lingered in everyone's mind. There were no *niñas* left in the household now. Only two *señoritas*, and one of them was the focus of a young man's amorous thoughts.

She closed the textbook, left it on the chair and went upstairs.

She found María Elena leaning close to the mirror above the dresser, pinching her nose with an instrument she had fashioned from a bottle cork and a piece of wire.

When María Elena saw Delia's reflection in the mirror, she quickly took off the homemade nose pincher and dropped it in a drawer. She swept the cork shavings from the top of the dresser into her cupped hand and dropped them in the wastebasket. She held Papá's pocketknife in front of her and flipped closed the blade with a grand gesture.

Perplexed by her sister's attitude and tired from the stress of dealing with Mamá's temperament, Delia felt the need to talk.

"What are you doing, Nena?"

"I invented a tool to shape my nose. A friend called me Ñatita, and I don't like it. So I am going to correct that."

Delia wanted to laugh, but thought better of it.

"How?"

María Elena pulled her invention out of the drawer. Two round slices of cork, each about one fourth of an inch thick, had been joined by inserting the ends of the U-shaped, three-inch long wire on the narrow edge of each piece of cork.

"See?" She pinched her nose between the cork wafers.

When she spoke again, María Elena's voice resonated in her nasal cavities and bounced back through her palate. Delia's choked giggle didn't get past her throat.

"I'll wear this to bed every night and soon my nose will not be as flat. It'll be reshaped, fine and upturned," María Elena said, looking in the mirror, moving her head from side to side, to better appreciate the results of her efforts.

"It is going to take more than a few nights, Nena. You were born with a flared nose. Wearing that device while you sleep isn't going to do it. Alberto Guzmán better get used to your flat nose, Ñatita."

Teasing María Elena took away some of the sting after Mamá appointed her as Delia's watchdog.

María Elena took off the nose pincher and tossed it on the dresser.

"By the way, this morning you were about to tell Mamá about Alberto, weren't you?"

She shook a finger at Delia.

"That would've been a bad move, you know. There are no witnesses. There is no evidence. Just your word against mine . . ."

She kept coming at Delia, poking her chest with her finger over and over again and Delia stepped back.

"And you *know* who Mamá believes. And if you don't tell, I won't be too hard on you and Juan Luis Rubio."

Angered, cornered against the footboard of her sister's bed, Delia blurted, "If you're not careful, Nena, one of these days there'll be evidence that you won't be able to hide by staying out of sight . . ."

She nudged María Elena's volatile nature further when she pulled out the front of her own skirt, implying a swollen belly.

Delia felt her sister's hot breath on her face, followed by blows on her shoulders. She put her arms in front of her face to ward off the attack and María Elena grabbed Delia's braid and forced her to fall backwards on the bed. Her feet kicked against the footboard as she wrestled to free her hair from María Elena's grasp.

María Elena's fist stopped in mid-air as they heard hard thumps on the floor coming from Juliana's room below theirs. The old servant hadn't hit the ceiling that way with the broom handle since they were little girls running in their room.

"You filthy pig!" María Elena whispered, loosening her grip on Delia.

Delia was sitting on her sister's bed and rubbing her shoulder when Juliana appeared at their door.

She looked from one to the other. "What's going on here, *niñas?*"

No answer. Juliana shook her head.

"You're lucky *Don* Nacho and *Doña* Berta went outside. This is shameful! Two *señoritas* fighting like rabble! What's the problem?"

María Elena held her hands behind her back and looked hard at Delia.

"No problem, Juliana, nothing that'll interest you. Nothing to bother Papá and Mamá about," María Elena declared. "Go on to bed. We'll be quiet."

Delia looked away when Juliana turned toward her and didn't move until she heard the door close and the sound of the woman's steps faded.

"Runt! Get off my bed!" María Elena shot. "How dare you suggest . . . Alberto is a gentleman."

"But does he care about you enough to talk to Papá? Does his family know about you two?"

María Elena started to turn down her bed and Delia couldn't avoid thinking of Mamá. Like her, María Elena could change moods at a snap of the fingers. When moments before she had been furious, now she seemed cool.

"I'm not going to discuss him with you. I don't care if the Rubios have come to talk to Papá. That means nothing. As for your rude gesture, I am still your older sister and you better show some respect."

It always came to that: the preeminence that came with her birth. But didn't its illegitimacy take away some of the inherent respect? And what of the respect she owed others, like her younger sister?

Delia dismissed her thoughts. It was useless to torture herself, and her head burned where her hair had been pulled. She touched her scalp and winced. She rotated her neck a few times and began to undress. A bruise had started to form on her shoulder.

She had gone too far this time with Nena and she would have to watch her steps with Juan Luis from now on, because María Elena would look for any reason to discredit her; but there would be nothing to tell. She wasn't that interested in carrying things further with Juan Luis at this point. She rather liked the idea that he would have to wait. If the poets were right, that would make him love her more. If Justo was right, Juan Luis Rubio's courage would be tested.

The following day, Delia walked out of the house into a bright breezy morning. Dew drops on the leaves of the lemon tree shined like diamonds on a green tray. A mockingbird practiced its repertoire, while hummingbirds and butterflies drank nectar from Mama's flowers. Delia sidestepped a puddle over the gravel near the gate. Last night, sleep had come in small segments strung together on a barbwire of frustration and resentment until she no longer could listen to her sister's peaceful breathing and went to lie on the sofa in the *sala*.

Walking to school, she recited to herself:

Si la flor delicada,
si la peña, que altiva no consiente
del tiempo ser hollada,
ambas me imitan, aunque variamente,
ya con fragilidad, ya con dureza,
mi dicha aquélla, y ésta mi firmeza.

She identified with Sor Juana Inés de la Cruz, whose poetry, so charged with pain and passion, caused the church of the seventeenth century to rebuke her. Delia wanted to sing out the nun's words this morning:

If the delicate flower,
if the rock, that proudly rejects
the imprint of time,
both are like me,
though differently,
now fragile, now hard,
that one my bliss, this one my strength.

She would find her own strength and she would make Mamá proud. Some day. As for her sister, knowing that she had pressured María Elena to be more discreet, gave Delia a small measure of satisfaction. For now, she would have the pleasure of showing Josefita Loma how María Elena planned to sharpen her nose for Alberto Guzmán.

Delia reached into her pocket and brought out the crude cork-and-wire gadget. She laughed out loud and quickened her step.

Chapter 13

The Pinedas celebrated Delia's sixteenth birthday with a weekend gathering at Coronado Beach. The Rubios and the Guzmáns, who owned beach homes in the resort, attended the birthday party along with Justo and his family.

The young people spent many hours in the early summer sun and under the watchful eyes of the adults. The times when they could play carefree, unchaperoned, had ceased when they reached puberty. It was the adults' way to remind young men to keep tight reins on their desires and to protect the honor and reputation of *señoritas* in the family. Besides, celebrations of life's cycles always included whole families. Delia's birthday was no different.

On Saturday afternoon, the Pinedas hosted a barbecue, with *lechón asado* as the main course. Juliana had basted the pig with her own special mixture of fragrant herbs and seasonings, and a succulent aroma wafted from the outdoor roasting pit, where fat dripped from the *lechón* onto the coals and sizzled.

Among the guests at Delia's birthday party were the Woolfords, an American couple who owned a vacation home adjacent to the house the Pinedas rented every time they stayed at Coronado Beach.

U.S. Air Force Colonel James Woolford's contribution to his country was entertainment. A self-styled comedian, Colonel Woolford ran the Officers Club at the Albrook air base, while his wife Betty rolled a bowling ball twice weekly as a member of two leagues at the Officers Club. She also played bridge several times during the week.

"There's so little to do around here," Betty Woolford lamented, "and this heat gives me rashes!"

Mamá had said that the Woolfords had a woman who arrived at the base every morning on the bus to clean their quarters and cook their meals. Another woman came two days a week to do their laundry by hand and iron their sheets and underwear.

"While Betty Woolford watches, nursing highballs," Juliana speculated bitterly, twisting her mouth in disdain.

After Delia blew out the candles on her birthday cake, the guests sat out in the shade of a *bohío* thatched with palm fronds. A gentle ocean breeze had started to cool the day, and Mrs. Woolford, slowly swinging in a hammock, finally stopped fanning herself.

The young people had gathered on the sand near the *bohío* and surrounded Alberto Guzmán, singing to the tunes he played on his guitar.

Colonel Woolford, drink in hand, walked up to them.

"Do you know 'September Song'?" he asked Alberto. "If you play it, I'll sing it for you kids."

Alberto stopped playing, stood up abruptly and thrust his guitar at Colonel Woolford.

"You play it, mister," Alberto snapped. "You play it with your Gold Roll hands!"

He had raised his voice and everyone heard him. His outburst left them speechless for a moment.

"What's eating him?" Delia heard Justo ask Isabel.

"I beg your pardon, young man!" Colonel Woolford said. He turned around and called to his wife. "Let's go, Betty. It seems we have overstayed our welcome."

Mamá and Papá stood up. So did *Don* Joaquín and *Doña* Mercedes Guzmán, Alberto's parents.

"I apologize for Alberto, Jim, please stay," Papá urged. "I don't believe he meant what he said—"

"I think he did, *Don* Nacho. That young man hasn't spoken to us all day. He's got a chip on his shoulder. We better go. Good night, *Don* Nacho, *Doña* Berta. No hard feelings."

"We hate to see you go, Jim. I'll get this straightened out. We are so sorry," Papá said.

The Woolfords walked away. Mamá and Papá watched them leave.

Delia saw that Alberto's parents had taken him aside and argued with him, while others whispered their embarrassment and dismay.

Alberto Guzmán approached Papá and Mamá, followed by his parents.

"I'm sorry," he simpered, and left without waiting for their answer. He didn't head for home. Instead, he walked down the long, solitary beach, then started to run, kicking sand with every step, his fists punching the air.

The Guzmáns looked very upset.

Don Joaquín spread his arms in a gesture of helplessness. "I'm sorry, everyone. Please don't let this spoil the day."

To Papá, he said, "Alberto has been talking a lot at home about the Americans. He complains about what a lousy deal they give the Panamanian employees in the Canal Zone. I know he's been attending political rallies behind our backs."

Doña Mercedes tried to justify her son. "It bothers him that the Americans come here and are placed in the Gold Roll and the Panamanians end up in the Silver Roll along with the colored Americans."

The Gold Roll included high-ranking military and civilian personnel. It meant superior housing, higher salaries, and access to the better facilities, including club houses and commissaries. The Silver Roll took in non-white Americans and Panamanian employees on a lower salary scale, and limited their access to housing, club houses, and commissaries.

Papá could barely contain his anger. "I don't care what his thoughts are. Those people were our guests. *I* am offended by Alberto's behavior."

Don Joaquín tried to calm him. "You know how it is, Nacho, once they enter the university, the kids start forming their own opinions. Lately, Alberto has been arguing with us all the time."

"That's not my problem," Papá insisted. "I just don't want anything like this to happen again. He owes them an apology."

"It won't happen again, Nacho." *Don* Joaquín placed a hand on Papá's shoulder. "I'll see that he apologizes to the colonel before we leave tomorrow."

Delia saw that María Elena followed Alberto Guzmán with her eyes. She looked as if her spirit had flowed from her to go and run alongside him. When he dove into a wave, she pressed her lips hard and shut her eyes.

"Those *universitarios* better find other excuses for their demonstrations," Papá said later that evening when Delia and María Elena walked with him on the beach. "The Gold Roll and the Silver Roll are being phased out. Just like racial segregation is going out of style in the United States. In another twenty years, in the seventies, things will be a lot different, *everywhere*."

"But it makes people mad, Papá," María Elena said. "It is our land they occupy. What gives them the right to such control?"

Delia suspected that María Elena had been listening to Alberto and had started to agree with his ideas.

"They lease and maintain the land, Nena, *that* gives them the right," Papá said. "We have a treaty with the Americans. If we want to change things, then the two governments need to negotiate. Running in the streets, destroying property and yelling '*Yanqui* go home' isn't the answer."

Delia said, "What's the fuss? Justo says that even the employees under the Silver Roll still make more money than people who don't work in the Canal Zone. When I graduate, that's where I am going to work." She picked up a piece of driftwood and brushed off the sand.

"You like the Americans because you go to their school," María Elena scoffed. "Every time we come to Coronado you run to talk to the *gringos*. I've seen you!"

"Why not? I talk to *gringos* all the time. You would too, if you had been accepted at my school. But you don't talk with Americans because the English the nuns teach you isn't good enough." As if she needed to needle her sister more, Delia added, "You couldn't work in the Canal Zone if you wanted to."

"That's enough, that's enough!" Papá gestured, waving his hands in front of him. He turned back toward the beach house. "I won't have you two arguing about it. It seems Alberto Guzmán managed to upset more than a *gringo*!"

Behind *Don* Nacho's back, Delia frowned, pursed her lips and shook her head to show her disapproval to María Elena.

111

A week later, Delia and Josefita walked across Santa Ana plaza on their way home from school. The old tree-shaded square seemed almost deserted, but for a few old men sitting on benches along flower-bordered paths and two young women standing on the steps of the church. Delia thought it odd. Even the kiosk near the bus stop was shuttered.

They crossed the street and stopped to look at new dresses displayed in a department store.

"Do you think your Mamá would make me that dress if I drew her a picture of it?" Josefita asked, pointing to a strapless, ruffled gown in the window. "That's called the New Look; straight from Paris!"

"Maybe . . . if she has time. She'll be sewing our new dresses for Christmas and New Year's Eve soon. Why don't you talk to—"

A distant rumble startled them.

They turned toward the noise and Delia saw the lottery vendor on the sidewalk in front of the store quickly gather her board and stool and run into a nearby alley.

Delia and Josefita watched a wave of people running on the street, advancing toward them. As the throng came closer, the tumult increased.

Traffic stopped in the middle of the street. Drivers shouted and honked their horns. Passengers rushed to leave buses and take cover, while demonstrators locked their arms together and forged ahead. Some carried banners, placards and Panamanian flags.

"*¡Panamá para los panameños! ¡Afuera los gringos! Yanqui* go home!" they shouted.

Young men and women ran, dodged cars, buses and trucks, pushing aside anyone who stood in their way.

Delia and Josefita flattened themselves against the store display window to avoid being trampled.

Delia saw a young man running, holding high the tricolor national flag. It flapped in the wind and, like a sail, it dropped and spread over the hood of a car when the youth who carried it stumbled and fell to the ground.

A young woman with bloodstains on her blouse picked up the flagstaff and continued running with it while the fallen standard-bearer scrambled toward the sidewalk.

The rapid clopping of horses' hooves, the rumble of motorcycles, and the hollow blast of handguns could be heard even before mounted policemen and motorcycle patrols came into view, just past the sudden cloud of tear gas that drifted up the street seeking victims.

Delia and Josefita trembled at the sound of glass shattering near them. They clutched their books, too terrified to move or to speak. Young men and women staggered past them, cursing, coughing, covering their faces. Others threw rocks at the police and shouted obscene insults while they wiped away tears and mucus.

Delia had started to feel the sting in her eyes from the cloud of tear gas when she saw María Elena running beside Alberto Guzmán. Before Delia could call to them, Josefita pulled at her arm and began to drag her into the store.

Delia managed to free herself from Josefita's grasp when she saw Alberto throw a bottle at a mounted policeman. She heard the bottle shatter on the pavement.

The horse reared up and the policeman launched a tear gas grenade toward Alberto.

The grenade hit the pavement, tear gas began to drift and Alberto ran away from it.

María Elena couldn't keep up with him. She stumbled and fell, the horse's hooves passing only a few feet away from her.

Delia dropped her books and ran toward María Elena. She zigzagged through the panicked throng, shouting, trying to make herself heard over the deafening noise of car horns, voices, hooves, gun blasts, sirens, and motorcycles.

Someone bumped into Delia and she was thrown into a spin. She could hardly see through the torrent of tears flowing from her eyes that felt as if they had been singed. She gasped for breath. She heard Josefita calling to her, but she kept going until she reached her sister.

María Elena struggled to get up.

"Nena! Nena! Come with me!" Delia shouted.

María Elena, overcome with tear gas, choking, reached her hands in front of her and Delia helped her up.

The two of them, barely able to keep their eyes open, fighting for every breath, held on to each other. Delia guided María Elena through the crowd toward the sound of Josefita's voice.

For a moment, Delia glanced back.

Alberto Guzmán was gone.

Josefita pounded on the door of the dress shop and a clerk let them in, locking the door behind them. She guided them through the store and to the stockroom in back. She took them to a lavatory and turned on the water faucet.

"Wash your face! Let water run on your eyes! I'll get something to wet down," the clerk said and reached for a box on the nearest shelf. She ripped off the top and handed new transparent nylon panties to each of the girls.

Josefita seemed to have suffered the least from the tear gas grenade. Her hands trembled when she held up the panties and started to laugh.

Delia held a pair of panties under the water faucet and placed the dripping undergarments over María Elena's face.

"What's so funny, Fita! What are you laughing about!" María Elena cried, her voice nasal, her throat clogged with mucus.

Josefita laughed even more.

The clerk wet another pair of panties and placed it over Delia's eyes. The flimsy nylon fabric didn't absorb water and it dripped, drenching the girls' white school uniforms.

Another clerk came in with face towels and the girls soaked those to wash their faces and soothe the sting in their eyes.

Josefita's hysterical laughter stopped suddenly.

"You're hurt, María Elena! You're bleeding!" Josefita screamed.

Delia took the cloth off her eyes and saw Josefita dabbing at the blood running down María Elena's legs.

María Elena looked at herself and her horrified eyes turned to Delia.

"Don't tell Mamá, Delia! Don't tell her! Please, Delia, don't tell Mamá!" she pleaded, crying, struggling to breathe.

"Stop it, Nena!" Delia yelled, afraid that María Elena would threaten to kill herself right there, in front of Josefita and the clerks, if Delia planned to tell Mamá that she had been in the demonstration with Alberto Guzmán. She turned to one of the women.

"Please call my father," she said between gasps and dabbing at her own eyes. She gave the clerk the phone number at the print shop. "And ask him to pick us up here."

"*Sí, señorita*, I'll do it right now."

"*Gracias*," Delia said.

The clerk went to place the call. She held a damp cloth over her nose and mouth. Some of the tear gas had leaked into the store.

María Elena sobbed.

Josefita raged, "Do you think your parents aren't going to see this? What were you doing in that demonstration, anyway, María Elena? Those were *universitarios*! You were running with Alberto Guzmán. Did he ask you to?"

María Elena covered her face and sobbed.

Delia touched Josefita's shoulder to get her attention and signaled her to be quiet.

The store's closed doors muffled the noise from the street. One of the clerks had collected the books that Delia and Josefita had dropped outside. She brought them in and stacked them on an empty shelf.

"I hope I got all your books," she said, "but there may be some torn pages. It's almost over out there. The cars are moving slowly, but there are some mounted guards and motorcycles going up and down the street. Come back out when you feel better."

Delia put her arm around the clerk. "Thank you for helping us."

The clerk shook her head. "It's not the first time we see these demonstrations, and it won't be the last." She seemed resigned to the demonstrations, the protests. "Today it is the *universitarios*. Tomorrow it may be the laborers on strike, or the teachers, or the police telling the president to move over and make room for their leader. At least this time they only broke one of our windows." She took a bloodstained washcloth from Josefita and dropped it in the sink with the rest of the wet cloths and panties. "I have to help outside. Stay here until you've calmed down," she told the girls.

When they were alone, Josefita looked at one sister, then the other. "What's going on? Why can't we tell what happened?"

María Elena squeezed shut her red, swollen eyes.

Delia turned to face the sink. She held on to the edge, her knuckles white. She kept her back turned to her sister.

"So what's the story going to be, María Elena?" Delia's anger was unmistakable.

Josefita blurted, "What story! We got caught in the demonstration, that's all! We weren't in it. Except for María Elena. Let her explain that!"

Delia turned around and shook Josefita's shoulders.

"Shut up! Shut up, Josefita! Please!"

When Delia turned to look at her sister, she saw a scared little rabbit.

María Elena held her arms tight around herself, her fingernails digging into the flesh. She trembled.

"We could say I was walking with you, that we met after school for a soda and we were walking home . . ." she whimpered.

Delia saw Josefita look up to the ceiling and blow air out of her pursed lips.

"Josefita, please, go along with this," Delia begged. "Believe me, you'll be saving me a lot of grief!"

"I don't understand any of this," Josefita fumed, "and I don't care to lie. So I'll just keep my mouth shut." She shook her index finger. "This time only. Don't expect me to do it ever again!"

Josefita slammed the door on her way out of the stockroom.

Delia's look measured María Elena slowly, from head to toe and back. She didn't know whether to feel pity or contempt. She had a headache. She imagined her head being held in a vise, María Elena twisting and tightening the screw. Delia had been thrown into this situation unwillingly and now had become an accomplice, dragged into a mudhole where María Elena wallowed. She hated herself for the lie that was to come.

"Stay here," Delia said, placing her hand gently on her sister's shoulder. "When Papá arrives, I'll come and get you."

She needed to get away from the small, suffocating room, away from María Elena. At the same time, the thought of what could have had happened to her sister out there in the street terrified her.

Delia waited for *Don* Nacho to arrive. She stood just inside the entry to the store, near Josefita. The two friends avoided looking at each other and watched the action on the street.

Cars and buses moved slowly, their drivers cautious, trying to avoid broken glass and sticks and rocks that lay on the pavement. Police cars and motorcycles cruised faster, sirens blaring, weaving among the other vehicles, like bullies flexing their muscles. The mounted patrols had moved on.

Store owners assessed damage and people watched from balconies, sometimes calling out to someone they recognized walking down the street. Wind blew along the street as if through a tunnel, carrying with it dust and debris. A rumpled strip of paper torn from a sign, with the phrase "*YANQUI* GO HOME," painted in red, tumbled on the pavement.

Papá parked in front of the store and stepped out of the car in a hurry. He hugged the girls and then held them at arms length.

"Are you hurt? You look like the tear gas got to you," he said, looking at their swollen faces.

"Some," Delia rushed to answer. "María Elena is inside, Papá." They walked into the store.

Delia and Josefita walked back toward the stockroom. *Don* Nacho followed them.

"María Elena? Was she with you? Is she all right?"

"She fell on broken glass, Papá. It cut her knees and her hands. But she's all right," Delia rushed to reply, as she sent Josefita a warning look.

Oh, God! How she hated to play María Elena's game!

Josefita frowned and pressed her lips together hard. She picked up the stack of books from the stockroom shelf.

When they came out of the stockroom, *Don* Nacho stopped to speak to one of the store clerks. He thanked her and insisted on paying for the damaged merchandise before he ushered the girls out of the store.

María Elena limped ahead of the others and sat in the back seat of the car. Josefita followed her, carrying the books. Delia sat in front with Papá.

Papá turned on the ignition and the car joined the rest of the slow-moving traffic.

"I had heard rumors about a demonstration," he said, "but I thought it would stay within the university campus, not come this far downtown. If I had known, I would have picked you up when school let out. I'm sorry."

Delia wanted to avoid explaining María Elena's presence. She had to distract Papá.

"What are the protesters demanding now, Papá?"

That's a dumb question, she thought, as if I didn't know, as if I hadn't seen the whole thing!

"It's about the American bases again. They want the American military out. These bums are listening to the communists!"

Delia had pushed the right button. Papá's anger would keep him talking and he would forget about María Elena.

Delia pressed on. "They don't ask themselves: if the military goes, who's going to protect the canal?"

"That's a good question. They don't want to admit that if the Americans go, the canal would be in jeopardy," Papá said.

"Justo said once that a lot of people would lose their jobs, too. That the canal keeps this country going."

"Not everyone says it out loud, but he's right. We are a melting pot of people, a crossroads for the world," Papá said.

Delia knew that Papá saw the American presence in Panamá as a blessing, not a curse. Unlike many others, Papá hadn't forgotten that the United States had helped Panamanians gain their independence from Colombia because the Americans wanted to finish the canal project—at which the French had failed. Papá counted many Americans among his friends and admired their leaders and their ideals of freedom and democracy. He wasn't active in politics, but

Delia knew that he strongly supported conservative candidates who often followed the U.S. government's lead.

They stopped and waited for a traffic policeman to wave them on.

Delia watched young people walking hurriedly, wiping their eyes, sniffling. A street vendor sorted through the oranges, avocados, papayas, and guavas spread on the sidewalk, salvaging fruit from his overturned cart.

A woman shouted from a balcony, to a man getting out of a car, "Where's he, Juan? Did you find him?"

"He's in the hospital! A horse stepped on him! He's got a broken leg!" the man shouted back.

"*¡Ave María Purísima!*" The woman yelled and ran back inside.

"Probably an innocent bystander," Papá said. "They won't be happy until a few lie dead on the street. I hope when you girls start at the university you won't rush to join political groups. Especially you, María Elena." He looked at her through the rear-view mirror. "You'll start there next term and I'll prefer that you concentrate on studying."

Your admonition might be a bit late, Papá, Delia thought.

A policeman waved them on and Delia quickly brought *Don* Nacho back to the subject of the demonstration.

"Do you think they'll succeed, Papá?"

"Who?"

"The *universitarios*. Do you think they have enough influence?"

"Only when they get representation in the assembly. When some of them decide to stop being perennial students and join the rest of us who work for a living and work through the system."

Delia heard an emergency siren approaching and Papá pulled closer to the curb to let an ambulance go by. He touched Delia on the arm and pointed his chin toward the sidewalk, where a boy spray-painted on a wall a misspelled obscenity.

"Stupidity," Papá said. "That's what all these demonstrations breed. It may happen one day that the *gringos* get tired of all this and, if the canal isn't that important to them anymore, they'll leave."

Papá's voice lowered, as if he were talking to himself. "And we'll all regret it . . ."

Papá pulled up by the gate at Josefita's house. She stepped out of the car, closed the rear passenger door and leaned toward *Don* Nacho.

"Thank you, *Don* Nacho," she said.

Don Nacho nodded, "*De nada*, Josefita, I'm glad you're all right."

Josefita turned toward the house, without a word to the Pineda sisters.

Don Nacho must have warned Mamá and Juliana that Delia had been caught in the mayhem of the demonstration, because the two women waited for them at the carport.

Mamá seemed surprised to see María Elena with them.

"Nena! You, too? I thought you were at Isabel's house," she said, rushing to take María Elena into the house.

"I was having sodas with Delia and Josefita," María Elena said, getting out of the car. Cool, as if she were reciting the gospel truth.

She got away with it, Delia thought, gathering up the books from the back seat.

When Delia went into the kitchen, María Elena already sat on a dining chair and Mamá placed gauze squares soaked in a boric acid solution on María Elena's closed eyelids.

"This will help soothe the inflammation," Mamá said. "Drink lots of water with lemon juice, *niñas*. That'll clear your throat."

Delia sat on a chair and let Juliana minister to her. She tried not to think. Tomorrow she would have to dance around Josefita's questions.

Then she remembered the agony she had felt when she saw María Elena fall and how she had responded, risking her own safety.

That must have been nearly two hours ago, she thought. I would have given my life for you then, Nena.

Chapter 14

The next day *Doña* Berta insisted that María Elena and Delia ride the bus to school. "The streetsweepers simply pile up the wreckage on the sidewalks and the landlords and shopkeepers don't clear it up fast enough," she said, making the beds in her daughters' room, while they finished dressing for school. "I don't want you girls to deal with that; a careless step can get you hurt."

Delia echoed her mother when she quipped, "Like yesterday, Nena would've been hurt worse if Josefita and I hadn't been around." She turned to her sister with a warning look. "You are getting careless."

María Elena lowered her eyes. "I don't know why so much is made of it. Demonstrations happen all the time. You can't always avoid them."

"You could've avoided the one yesterday if you had gone to Isabel's house like you said you would," Mamá said, "Now hurry up, or you'll miss your bus!"

Delia stopped braiding her hair for a moment. She had detected suspicion and reproach in her mother's voice.

Did she catch the lie in the excuse María Elena had given for being in the middle of the melee the day before?

"Fools!" Papá blurted.

They were having breakfast and the stories on the front page of *La Estrella* wound him up again. "Wasting their time with politics. If they don't want to study for a degree, then let them get a job. Let some deserving youths put scholarships to good use! Many of those demonstrators are on scholarships their parents got for them because they have friends in the government, not because they are academic stars."

"Do you thing Alberto Guzmán is one of them, Papá?" Delia had asked, taking advantage of *Don* Nacho's remarks to get back at her sister.

121

María Elena didn't look up from her bowl of oatmeal, but she blushed and the spoon shook slightly in her hand.

"Is he one of what?" Papá took a sip of steaming coffee.

"One of the revolutionaries," Delia said.

Papá chuckled. "Can't tell for sure if he's a true revolutionary. Although he acted like one at Coronado Beach. He doesn't like the *gringos*, but I don't know if he would join the march against them."

María Elena cleared her throat and stared at Delia.

Delia bit off a piece of toast and wondered. If Papá knew that Alberto Guzmán had been in the march and that María Elena was there with him, would he throw her out of the house? And what about Delia? Papá wouldn't forgive her lie. She didn't want to risk that.

"Well, then, do you think he's an academic star?" she continued innocently.

"Hmm . . ." Papá looked up to the ceiling and pondered Delia's question, then shrugged. "I've never heard Joaquín brag about Alberto's academic triumphs, if there were any. Why do you ask?"

"Just curious. Some girls I know think he's something special," Delia said.

Mamá poured more hot chocolate for Delia and she sounded annoyed when she asked, "Are you discussing young men with your friends already?"

Delia backed off. "Not really, Mamá, I just heard them." She turned toward María Elena. "I think they were some of your friends, Nena, right?"

María Elena stood up. "I haven't heard any such talk." She turned to her mother. "I'll be late if I don't hurry."

Mamá kissed her cheek and Papá nodded, excusing María Elena from the breakfast table. With her sister gone, Delia dropped the subject of Alberto Guzmán.

Delia heard her sister slam the gate. She shook her head. "She's late as usual." It didn't matter. The bus driver would wait for her and then go on past suburban streets shaded by acacias; past mansions protected by walls topped with shards of bottle glass that reflected the morning sun. Delia saw the wall that surrounded the all-girls nun's school as overkill. After all, for a place so populated with praying souls, the wings of angels should be sufficient armor against evil intrusion.

While Delia waited for her own bus, she watched the passengers in other buses. The ones that made the University campus run carried a few of the students who had participated in the march the day before. They wore their bandages like badges of honor.

Delia's bus was almost full, with one empty seat next to Josefita. Delia's other choice was a window seat near the back next to a large woman who had already been to the market. The smell of raw meat and shrimp emanating from the overflowing straw bag she held on her lap gave her away.

"Good morning, Fita," Delia said, taking the seat next to her friend.

Josefita only nodded and turned to look out the window.

They rode in silence for a few blocks and soon the driver turned on the radio. He fiddled with the dial at full volume. The fragments of music, news, and announcements blasted out as if to drown the noise from outside: the racket from radios blaring in other buses and cars, dogs barking, street vendors shouting, glass being swept from sidewalks.

This bus didn't meander through quiet suburban tree-shaded streets. It crawled through the pulsing main artery in the city that ended at the shore of the Pacific Ocean, a block from the American Methodist high school that Delia and Josefita attended. Once, in a dream, Delia had seen a giant broom sweeping a flailing and moaning mass of humanity down the same avenue and right out into the ocean.

When Delia and Josefita got off the bus, they didn't go beyond a wall into a secluded compound. They walked up to the unfenced front yard of the Methodist church behind which the three-storied school building stood.

Some of the four hundred young men and women that populated the high school mingled in groups under the few citrus and palm trees that dotted the yard, and along the sea wall which bore the scars from past hurricanes that had slammed the ocean waves against it.

The modest looks of the American Methodist School disguised the high quality of bilingual teaching that took place there, and the high standard of academic performance required of the students. AMS didn't gather the children of well-to-do parents in its classrooms, nor did its tuition match that of the School of the Immaculate Conception of Mary that María Elena attended.

Josefita walked ahead of Delia and joined a cluster of their friends standing under the shade of a lemon tree.

She's still angry about yesterday, Delia gathered. It saddened her. Josefita Loma had been her friend since they shared a desk for two in the first grade. Outside the Pineda home, Delia shared more of her life with Josefita than with María Elena.

At that moment, Delia heard a few notes played on a trumpet and her spirits lifted.

Juan Luis Rubio played in the school band and had taken to playing the same notes on his trumpet each time he saw Delia from a distance. They were the beginning notes of a song, a song about pearls a woman kept in a beautiful case of crimson velvet, and a man's longing to count them, kiss by kiss.

Delia waved to Juan Luis. The loud buzzer that signaled the start of the school day called her away from him. She caught up with Josefita and touched her arm.

"We need to talk. I know you are angry at me because of María Elena, but I can explain," Delia whispered.

"After the second period, I'll be at the library," Josefita said. "You can look for me there."

Delia wished the school library had been located towards the front of the building. Back here, facing the Bay of Panamá, the cramped space where the students did research and whispered gossip smelled of seaweed, dead fish, and musty books, more so when the windows were wide open to let in the sea air.

Delia found Josefita bent over a couple of heavy tomes.

When Delia sat across from her, Josefita looked up and arched an eyebrow.

"It stinks!" Josefita said.

"It always stinks! The tide brings a lot of garbage from those ships that cross the Canal."

"That's not what I'm talking about. It's *yesterday* that stinks. You covering up for Nena."

"You don't understand," Delia pleaded.

"Oh, yes, I do. I understand that María Elena gets in trouble and you front for her. You've done that for years now. Delia, you've got to stop it. You are not little girls anymore."

Josefita stood up and went to the window. Then she turned around to face Delia. With the sunlight behind her, Josefita's curly hair took a coppery glow. Her face was in shadows and it bothered Delia that she couldn't see it. On the other hand, it was easier to talk to Josefita this way. It was like going to confession, with the priest behind the curtained grill. Even if you could tell who it was by his voice, not seeing his reaction made it easier to confess the sin.

"María Elena gets emotional. She is very afraid of Mamá," Delia said.

"No, Delia. She's not afraid of *Doña* Berta. *Doña* Berta wouldn't lay a hand on her. You've told me that yourself. I think all Nena wants is to be your Mamá's angel. The one who can do no wrong. And you're helping her at your own expense. Why? I don't understand. Why, Delia?" Josefita threw up her hands.

Delia laced her fingers over the table and her knuckles turned white. She wanted to tell Josefita that María Elena was only her half sister. That she felt sorry for her because Pablo Luis Morán had denied her his name. That there was a secret in the Pineda home like a persistent bad dream from which no one knew how to awaken. Her fingers tightened into a fist that hurt, reminding her that she was to uphold the Pineda traditional reserve.

"I thought we were going to talk, Delia," Josefita pressed.

"She threatens to kill herself if I tell Mamá what she does wrong!" Delia blurted and immediately regretted her indiscretion.

"What!" Josefita said a bit too loudly and they heard Mrs. Wilson, the librarian, shushing them from her desk.

"Please, Josefita, I can deal with it," Delia whispered.

Josefita sat down again and leaned towards Delia.

"Do you think she would do it?" she whispered, her question colored with curiosity and incredulity.

"I don't know . . . I am afraid to find out."

Josefita let out a soft whistle.

The two friends looked at each other. Delia searched Josefita's eyes for a promise to keep the confidence. She wished she could take back her words.

After a while, Josefita said, "Did you ever hear the saying, '*O corres, o te encaramas*'?"

Delia shook her head. She hadn't heard Papá use that one yet.

"It has to do with wild horses. It means either you run away from them and lose them, or you get on them and tame them."

"It means taking risks," Delia said, looking at her fingers still locked together.

Josefita placed her hands gently over Delia's.

"Yes. And we are old enough to start taking risks. My mother said that when a girl becomes a *señorita*, she becomes responsible for what she does. I don't think Nena is taking responsibility for her acts if you help her lie." Josefita paused, then, impatiently added, "She's a senior about to graduate, Delia. She isn't helpless!"

Delia's eyes were fixed on Josefita. Her friend was revealing a new side of herself. This wasn't the Josefita who loved to gossip, who vexed teachers with a twisted sense of humor that not too long ago drove her to sneak under the librarian's desk and snatch away the shoes the mild-mannered spinster had the habit of taking off. Josefita had managed to hang Mrs. Wilson's lace-up oxfords on a high branch of an orange tree outside the school building, and classmates gathered to watch a janitor retrieve them while Mrs. Wilson stood at the door in her stockings.

Delia felt Josefita's kindness and concern, but it wasn't enough to move Delia to betray the Pineda reserve.

The buzzer signaling the start of a class period cracked the tension of the moment and released her. Josefita squeezed Delia's hands before she stood up and began to gather her books.

"Don't let her do this to you, Delia. You don't deserve it," she said and walked out of the library.

Delia stood at the window that had framed Josefita's silhouette. She heard the school band members tuning their instruments. They practiced in the school basement, built on the beach, that at different times served as auditorium, band room, and basketball court. The ocean tides determined the schedule of activities, because it was impossible to hold assemblies and band rehearsals when the surf crashed against the basement's walls.

Delia heard the clear sound of Juan Luis Rubio's trumpet. She looked at fishing boats bobbing in the distance. It was low tide.

"It really stinks," she whispered, and bit her lip.

Chapter 15

Delia climbed the stairs to Justo's and Isabel's apartment, glad to be inside a building and in the shade. She had walked several blocks in the mid-December sun, stopping to look at Christmas merchandise in store windows and making mental notes about items to suggest to Mamá.

She had noticed more plastic than celluloid in imported toys and trinkets. She had looked at dolls in store displays and recalled that she still owned one of the few she had ever received as Christmas presents from her parents. María Elena had bashed in the doll's face once during one of her fits of anger and Delia had managed to repair it, pushing out the doll's thin celluloid cheeks, but it was not the same. Telltale cracks remained as faded lines, like the scar on her own right hand where María Elena had dripped hot caramel many years ago.

The *clap-clap-clap* of an electric toy train greeted her when she entered the Salazar's apartment. She almost dropped the box she carried when Toñito bumped into her.

"Look, Delia, it's finished!" he said, his arms opened wide, as if to encircle the source of the noises.

The train traveled on a narrow track through the landscape of a Nativity scene born of Isabel's imagination and Toñito's whims. It occupied a good portion of the small living room, resting four feet off the floor on a large piece of plywood painted white. A celestial blue length of oilcloth tacked to the wall had been disguised with pieces of cotton glued on to look like clouds, giving the illusion of a night sky. Holes punched on the oilcloth allowed tiny lightbulbs to shine through, resembling the constellations.

Isabel came in from the kitchen, tying on an old apron.

"It's been a lot of work, so we hope you approve," she said.

María Elena and Isabel had spent nearly two weeks creating a *papier-mâché* village, complete with snowy mountains overlooking a desert. In an oasis, a small mirror reflected palm trees made of green and brown crêpe paper and a pair of celluloid camels seemed to be drinking from the illusory pond. Painted cardboard houses bordered miniature roads of poured sand and tiny pebbles. Little lights shone through the cellophane-covered windows. At the highest corner against the blue sky, a stable awaited the Holy Family. Over the thatched roof, an angel in white silk and golden halo held a banner: *"Gloria in Excelsis Deo."*

"I made the star!" Toñito said, pointing to a six-pointed star fashioned from aluminum foil.

The most luxurious items in the Nativity scene so far were the three Magi. Their shiny satin robes and the gold leaf that covered the boxes bearing their gifts glinted in sunlight that came through the open door. The Pinedas had given them to Toñito for his first Christmas nearly six years ago.

"So what do you think?" Toñito tugged on Delia's skirt.

"Splendid! Amazing!" she applauded.

Then she turned toward Isabel. "A train?"

Isabel held out her hands and shrugged. "I tried to dissuade him. But I lost again. He argued that there were too many mountains for the Magi to climb on foot."

She took from Delia the box of Christmas ornaments *Doña* Berta was contributing to the Salazar family Christmas tree and placed it on a table.

They went in the kitchen. Isabel poured more rum on the fruit mixture she had prepared two months before and kept in a large glass jar, soaking in the spirits. That was the main ingredient in the Salazar family's holiday gift for friends: the moist fruitcake that Isabel baked and wrapped in wax paper before placing it in decorated straw baskets, a carryover from Ana's time, like the ointments Isabel now used to comfort her husband and child.

She covered the jar tightly and returned it to a shelf.

"If it wasn't for Toñito, this would be a very sad Christmas for me," she said. "The first without my Mamá. I had no desire to decorate, or celebrate. But Justo convinced me that it would not be fair to Toñito if we ignored the holiday. Then, all the preparations for the Nativity scene seemed to take away the sadness. It is as if God is reminding me that, although he took Mamá from me, he has given me a husband and a child to love."

Delia had heard Juliana pass judgment on Isabel's marriage soon after the wedding. "It won't last," the servant had said, "it's a 'have-to' thing. He didn't offer before the child started to grow inside her. Besides, she isn't an experienced woman. How does she know he's the one man for her? There's always the chance she might meet someone else and then, who knows? After all, she's Ana's child!"

But Juliana had been wrong again. It seemed that, when it came to Ana's family, Juliana could throw her predictions out the window.

Isabel took a tray from the freezer and ran water over it to loosen ice cubes. She put some in two tall glass mugs and poured pineapple juice over them. She reached in a window planter and pinched some mint, then floated the dark green, fragrant leaves in the drinks.

Delia's eyes followed Isabel's graceful movements. She wore a white cotton dress at home; but when she went out on errands or on limited social gatherings, Isabel wore mourning black. She would for at least a year longer.

Would she ever feel such sorrow if Mamá died? Isabel had been Ana's special child. Mamá's special child was María Elena.

From where they sat, they watched Toñito turning the toy train on and off. He would let it run for a few moments, then carefully flip the switch to stop the train. Once, his hand brushed against the figure of a shepherd and toppled it. Toñito caught his breath and looked toward his mother.

"Just pick it up, *hijo*," Isabel smiled. "It won't break."

"I'll remind Justo to get more batteries for that train. I don't think those will last until Christmas at the rate Toñito keeps the train running," Delia said.

Isabel looked at her son and sadness crept into her voice when she said, "He asked me if his *abuelita* will celebrate Christmas in Heaven with the angels. I said yes."

"I know he misses Ana. We all do," Delia said. "I'm glad you are bringing him to hear the Christmas concert at the school. It'll cheer everyone up."

"I heard Juan Luis Rubio is playing a trumpet solo."

Isabel's unexpected comment caught Delia by surprise.

"News travel fast. Josefita told you?"

Isabel nodded. "Exciting, isn't it?"

"He's very good at it. *Doña* Chabela says that his love for music comes from his Italian side," Delia said.

"I had my first boyfriend when I was sixteen, too."

"He's not my boyfriend yet."

"He's talked to *Don* Nacho, Delia, that counts. And when the time comes, you two will be *novios*. Like I was saying, I had a boyfriend. But he wasn't like Juan Luis at all. He cut corners, so to speak. Mario didn't bother with introductions or love letters. He just followed me one day and, when we were alone, grabbed my arm, turned me around, and kissed me."

Delia opened her eyes wide, swallowed the mouthful of fruit juice, then joined in Isabel's laughter.

"Of course, I never told Mamá. She would've sent my brothers to handle Mario!"

"Did you care for him?"

"No. But it was nice to feel wanted."

"How did it feel?"

"Being wanted?"

"No. The kiss!"

Isabel sipped some juice. "Oh, I don't know," she shrugged. "All I remember is that I did what I was supposed to do. I slapped Mario!"

Their burst of laughter interrupted a hummingbird's lunch and the bird buzzed away from the window planter. In the *sala,* the toy train chugged.

Delia leaned closer to Isabel and whispered, "Was it a dry kiss, or a soul kiss?"

Isabel looked at her as if deciding whether to answer.

Delia didn't blink. She saw no lack of decorum in her question.

"It must have been a soul kiss. I wanted to vomit afterwards. By the way, where do you get all the information?" Isabel squinted at Delia.

"I read."

Isabel tilted her head and winked.

"Is that so?"

"Yes. That's so." Delia waved a hand. "Don't worry. At the rate I am going, the experience isn't knocking at my door. Papá has forbidden us to meet in private and Mamá set up Nena as my bodyguard," Delia twisted her mouth in disgust.

"That's all right," Isabel said. She watched Toñito playing in the *sala*. "You don't want to rush into things. It's best to sidestep regret."

"Do you have regrets?"

"Oh, no! Justo would give his life for us. He loves us that much."

Isabel was twenty when she had moved in with Justo and Delia had heard Juliana telling Mamá that Isabel couldn't claim ignorance as an excuse.

If Isabel knew that much about her, maybe she knew about Nena and Alberto Guzmán.

"Do you know that María Elena sees Alberto?" Delia knew she sounded gossipy, but she hoped to draw a confidence from Isabel.

"They don't *see* each other. They are just friends, Delia. Besides, María Elena is already eighteen and Alberto is twenty. He comes from a distinguished family. If he were interested in being Nena's *novio*, he would have spoken to *Don* Nacho already."

Isabel stood up and called Toñito into the kitchen.

So, Delia conjectured, as much as María Elena seems to spend time with Isabel, when it comes to Alberto, Nena doesn't confide in her. Isabel doesn't sound like an accomplice.

Isabel poured milk into an aluminum cup, cut a piece of *bollo*, placed the flavored corn dough wrapped in husks on a plate and set a place for Toñito at the kitchen table. She steadied the chair for him when he came to eat the snack.

Toñito displayed his milk mustache to Delia. She smiled, but her thoughts were elsewhere.

María Elena wasn't bluffing. There were no witnesses, no evidence of her closeness to Alberto. And if anyone suspected them, they were not willing to admit it. Those two were being too careful to be innocent. And how serious could Alberto be since he had not spoken to Papá about courting María Elena?

Isabel interrupted Delia's musing. "Do you know when the Christmas trees will arrive at the dock? I would like to have one without dried needles."

"Mamá said we would pick up ours on the twenty-second and leave it in a bucket of water until Christmas Eve. Would you like us to bring yours then, also?"

"Yes, would you?"

Isabel went into the bedroom and came back with her purse. She pulled some Balboas out of her wallet.

"I think this will cover it. If there is anything left over, please bring me some mistletoe."

Delia stood up, took the money from Isabel and set her empty glass in the kitchen sink. She stopped to hug Toñito and pinched a morsel from his plate.

"Hmm, delicious!"

"You want some milk?" Toñito offered her his half filled cup.

"No, thanks, people will laugh at me if I walk around with a milk mustache."

Delia and Isabel walked toward the door.

"So you want mistletoe? For kisses? Wouldn't you rather have a new gold necklace, or a pearl ring?" Delia asked.

"If you find a sprig of something that would suggest that, bring it, too; but I'm more likely to get kisses," Isabel said, as Delia began descending the steps towards the street.

She waved without looking back.

When Delia arrived at the Pineda house, she entered through the front door. She liked to come in and see the Pineda's Nativity scene in the *sala*, placed so it could be seen from the entry courtyard. Every year Mamá added figures and buildings to the original

Italian porcelain display that she had inherited from *Abuela*. She had been careful to preserve the look of antiquity, staying away from modern miniature houses. Or trains, Heaven forbid.

One of Papá's Jesuit friends had painted a new background this year. It carried the illusion from the rest of the display, with the foothills of Bethlehem blending in the distance with the resplendent night sky.

Mamá had three sets of Magi, which she changed as they progressed on their trek to Bethlehem. First they rode their camels, then they were on foot and looked toward the star. The last set she placed next to the manger on January 6, Epiphany, when the church observed the arrival of the Wise Men at the stable where the *Niño Dios* was worshiped. On that day, the Magi knelt next to the manger in their most elaborate robes and headdresses. They offered to the Christ-child gifts in gilded boxes encrusted with tiny translucent colored stones.

Every year the Pineda family's Nativity scene would start taking shape promptly on December 10, and four days later it was ready for viewing, complete with background music and a stream that, with the help of a small pump, meandered throughout. Each night, Papá left the front gate open so anyone could enter at will to admire the Nativity from the window, then go on to see other displays in the neighborhood. Some would stop long enough to chat, or have a cup of hot chocolate flavored with cinnamon and served by Juliana in china cups.

"The Christmas tree we could do without," Papá had said. For him, it was still a foreign tradition that detracted from the true meaning of Christmas. He took a particular dislike to the trees, covered with artificial snowflakes, that had appeared in the stores the year before.

"It will really be a cold day in Hell when we see snow in Panamá City. There wasn't snow in Bethlehem either. So why decorate with fake stuff? Leave that to the Americans who are homesick!" Papá had said.

He gave in to pressure time and again, when his daughters insisted on putting up a Christmas tree.

"It would welcome visitors," María Elena had said, "And it would look magical on New Year's Eve."

"And you better take it down right after!" Papá insisted, somewhat appeased. But he prevailed to a point, because the tree was not allowed in the house until Christmas Eve when María Elena and Delia invited a few friends to help test and hang the strings of colored lights; the glass, celluloid, and handmade ornaments.

Delia found María Elena in the kitchen helping Juliana shell walnuts.

"Isabel would like us to get her Christmas tree at the same time we get ours," she said to María Elena.

"Did she give you the money to pay for it?"

"Yes. If there's any left, she'd like some mistletoe," Delia said handing Isabel's money to her sister.

María Elena lifted a bowl of shelled walnuts from her lap and placed it on the kitchen table.

"She'll get some anyway. We'll have more than we need," she said, and shook the skirt of her dress, letting bits and pieces of walnut shell fall to the floor.

Juliana began to sweep.

"You be careful where you put that mistletoe, *niñas*," Juliana said. "If *Don* Nacho catches some boy kissing you on Christmas Eve, that'll be the end of the party."

The two sisters looked at each other. María Elena opened her mouth in mock surprise and Delia laughed.

María Elena kept up the fun. She placed her hands on her face, planted herself in front of Juliana and brought her face close to the servant.

"Juliana! What do you take us for? *¿Vagabundas?*"

Juliana brushed her aside, picked up the bowl María Elena had left on the table, then turned around. She was serious and spoke softly.

"Watch what you say, *niña* Nena, I didn't use that word. I'm just warning you. Don't let *Don* Nacho catch you."

Has she seen her? Delia wondered, she knows something is going on.

María Elena put an arm around Juliana. "You worry too much. Can you remember when was the last time Mamá and Papá had reason to be angry with us?

"Maybe not with you, *niña*. But not very long ago *Doña* Berta was upset when *niño* Juan Luis wrote a letter to your sister."

"Ah, yes," María Elena turned toward Delia. "You must watch your step, Delia. Better yet, I'll watch your step," she teased.

María Elena looked happy. She had kept up her grades and seemed undaunted by the final exams that would follow after the holidays. She had been admitted to the university, and would start attending classes the following term. Papá had given her the option to study in Mexico or Argentina, but she wanted to remain close to home, she had said. This overflowed Mamá's cup of joy. Her daughter would remain close to her supervision, an example to Delia, she had said with moist eyes. "She's a good daughter."

"Watch my step," Delia muttered to herself as she went up the stairs to their room. "She'll be trying to walk on quicksand in a few months." A voice in her head added: *And sucking you in with her . . .*

Chapter 16

This year Alberto Guzmán was back among those invited to decorate the Pineda family Christmas tree. So was Juan Luis Rubio, who telegraphed his love to Delia with looks that caressed her, enigmatic smiles that drew nervous laughter from her, and raised eyebrows that scared her a little because she read in them an urgent "When?" When would she dare to ignore Papá's rules?

When she offered him a tray of pastries, the warm touch of his hand struck lightning through her. She felt a fever rising from the bottom of her feet, as if her shoes had disappeared and she had stepped on the burning coals of a *fogón*.

She turned away quickly, her face aflame.

When she looked back at him, Juan Luis was serious, his eyes still fixed on her.

He looked around, then mouthed, *"Te quiero."*

¡Madre mía!, Delia invoked, hold me up! It would be so sweet to hear those words close to her ear, with his arms around her, like she'd been dreaming so much lately. Only in her dreams he said *"Te quiero, mi amor"* instead.

The sound of Alberto Guzman's guitar brought her back. The others, including María Elena, had started to sing a Christmas carol. She walked away from Juan Luis, but she could feel his eyes following her, passing through the back of her neck and down to her chest and she sighed.

Delia wondered if her eyes shone brighter after that instant with Juan Luis, as María Elena's did when she looked at Alberto Guzmán. Even when they were not standing together, Nena and Alberto seemed linked by some invisible bond. Delia knew she wasn't imagining things. She saw him sneak a kiss on the corner of María Elena's mouth when he came in and she was standing under the mistletoe.

Mamá and Papá had gone to take the Christmas presents to Justo and his family, and Nena had made herself available for Alberto's kiss when Juliana went into the kitchen.

Josefita had noticed, too. Or perhaps, she was more aware since she'd helped Delia raise a smokescreen to protect María Elena during the demonstration.

"I don't think Alberto can eat," Josefita said when she helped Delia place *bizcochos* on a tray. "He's already having trouble keeping his eyes off María Elena. I bet he'll be talking to *Don* Nacho soon."

Delia didn't answer. She knew better than to discuss her sister with Josefita, who already knew too much. Delia would keep her mouth shut, no matter how much the knowledge peeved her that Alberto Guzmán was wearing Mamá's medallion beneath his buttoned-up dress shirt and tie.

Juan Luis stood beside her when the Christmas tree lights were turned on.

"I've left a gift for you in the garden, under the bench beneath the lemon tree," he whispered.

"You shouldn't—" she began, but seeing his resolve underscored by his uplifted chin and sly smile, all she could do was thank him.

Later, filled with guilt, feeling like a thief, Delia found a small package wrapped in gold foil and a narrow white ribbon in the garden and hid it, unopened, in one of her dresser drawers.

The young people finished with the Pineda's tree in time to join their families at the cathedral for the *Misa del Gallo*. When Delia was a child, Mamá had told her that the rooster crowed at midnight when Jesus was born, but Delia had never heard a mystic *cock-a-doodle-doo* during the Mass. Something was missing.

At the church, baskets decorated with golden ribbon held tubs planted with poinsettia and amaryllis. Garlands of orange and lemon leaves, white roses and carnations decorated the altar and the niches where time-worn images of the saints glowed by candlelight.

Across the aisle, a fidgety Toñito sat between Justo and Isabel. Delia caught his eye and winked at him.

Toñito leaned over and waved at her. Justo caught him by the waist before he fell against the back of the pew in front of them.

From then on, Justo kept his arm around Toñito's shoulder to quiet him.

Delia stopped looking around and fixed her eyes on the main altar. She knew the Rubios were seated a few pews behind them. *Doña* Chabela Rubio prayed in distinct whispers and her fervor sometimes drew the attention from those around her. Delia fought the urge to look back and seek Juan Luis. On the other hand, María Elena didn't have to turn around. The Guzmáns were seated in a pew across the aisle and toward the front. Delia saw her sister glance in that direction several times. Alberto never looked back.

Mamá and Papá followed the Latin ritual repeating prayers from a shared missal and their devotion seemed to unite and isolate them from their surroundings.

The scented smoke, from burning frankincense, myrrh, and candles, almost overcame Delia. She closed her eyes and imagined herself soaring as the organ music rose to the domed ceiling and bounced off the frescos depicting saints, angels and martyrs in a heaven born of an artist's vision of God's throne.

Enraptured, she listened to the nuns in the choirloft sing "Gloria!" and "Hallelujah!" The cathedral's bells tolled a joyous hymn of triumph in the still, cool night, proclaiming the Savior's birth. It was midnight, though the rooster didn't crow.

The Pinedas joined in the long line of believers kneeling in front of the priest, who held a life-size image of the baby Jesus. From the loft came the melody of a sweet lullaby.

Delia looked into the depth of the innocent glass eyes of the *Niño Dios* and kissed the delicate foot. "Forgive me, Jesus, bless me," she prayed silently, the remnants of the trepidation brought about by sneaking in the garden earlier pulled at her conscience. Peace embraced her and she imagined herself wrapped in the wings of angels.

Before the Pinedas went to Mass, Mamá had placed the kneeling porcelain figure of Mary next to the manger lined with fresh straw. On the opposite side, Joseph stood, leaning on a staff. A glowing angel, blowing a long golden trumpet, extended its wings over the roof of the stable that sheltered the Holy Family.

After their return from *Misa del Gallo*, and before the Christmas dinner was served, Papá handed the pink porcelain figure of baby Jesus to Mamá. She closed her eyes briefly, kissed the holy image, gave it to María Elena who repeated Mamá's motion and handed it to Delia.

She held the figure tenderly in her hands, made a wish, kissed it, and gave it back to Papá.

"Father, we pray that your peace will enter this home and that your blessings will fill every corner. We thank you, Lord for the gift of your child and we humbly celebrate his birth," Papá said, as he placed the image of a robust baby Jesus with raised feet and opened arms on the straw of the manger.

"Amen," the Pinedas said in unison, crossing themselves.

Juliana was spending the holidays in the interior with her family and Mamá had cooked dinner with the help of María Elena and Delia. With a flourish and bowing to the applause of her family, Mamá served the golden roasted chicken stuffed with apples, nuts and raisins. Then brought in the rice with coconut, potato and beet salad, steamed asparagus with almonds, and bananas baked in caramel and spices.

Papá opened a bottle of champagne and, when it was time for dessert, flambéed the bananas with cognac.

"May we open one present now, Papá?" María Elena tilted her head downward, her hazel eyes quizzing *Don* Nacho in the charming way that had always resulted in Papá giving in to her wishes.

"Are you trying to make a tradition of it, Nena? Last year you got away with it," Papá said, and took another sip of his *café au lait*.

Delia chimed in, "I think that's a good tradition, Papá. After all, we know what we asked for, and we don't wait until Día de Reyes, like when we were little."

Papá looked to Mamá for an opinion. "Are you raising greedy daughters, *mi amor*?"

"If they open a present now, perhaps we can sleep a little later in the morning," Mamá said, leaning her head on Papá's shoulder as Delia and María Elena bolted from the table laughing. Each took a box from under the Christmas tree.

María Elena unwrapped hers first: a plain mahogany jewelry box. As the others watched, she undid the small brass latch. Inside, on the black velvet lining, rested a long flat *cadena chata*, two gold and pearl *peinetas*, and a dozen hair pins adorned with coiled gold springs and pearl flowers.

Her jaw dropped. She lifted the chain and caressed the wide, flat links; then let them fall slowly, one over the other, as she put the chain back in the jewelry box. She set it on a table. Mamá and Papá stood at the door to the *sala* and María Elena went over, kissed them and hugged them.

"*¡Gracias!* It's all so beautiful!" she said.

This jewelry had been promised to her on her eighteenth birthday. That day her parents had given her the traditional *pollera* dress, handmade to order. The fine white linen was appliquéd with purple flowers on each of the ample ruffles that were joined with handmade *mundillo* lace.

María Elena picked up the box, admiring its contents. "So beautiful!" she said, and hung the chain around her neck. She fingered the gold fish pendant joined in sections so it moved as if it were swimming. She stuck some of the jeweled pins on her short hair, and finished placing the combs on each side. One of the combs slid down and she caught it before it fell to the floor. The pearl flowers on gold springs attached to the pins shimmered and trembled as she turned her head this way and that.

"It's my turn," Delia said, tearing the wrapping off a large box.

Don Nacho reached into his pocket, pulled out the blade of a small knife, and cut the strapping tape that held the top flaps of the box together.

When Delia saw the black case, she knew that Papá had come through for her again. She had hinted for a portable Smith-Corona typewriter when Justo asked her what she wished for this Christmas. Papá got the word. She delayed opening the case. She went to where her father stood.

"*Gracias*, Papá!" Delia said, unable to find other words to express the depth of her gratitude. She felt such tenderness toward her father, she was afraid she would cry when she put her arms around him and kissed his cheek.

Mamá handed her another package.

"We want to see you do more than just practice your typing lessons, *hija*, we know how much you like to read other people's words. Now you can start putting down your own."

Delia unwrapped a box of crisp linen bond paper tied with a blue ribbon and printed with a letterhead: "Delia Susana Pineda." She caressed the top page, raised her eyes to look at her parents again, holding the stack of paper close to her chest, and kissed her mother.

"*Gracias*, Mamá. I'll write my first poem for you," she promised.

Doña Berta nodded and began to gather their empty cups.

"Time for bed, *niñas*. We'll open the rest of the gifts in the morning," *Don* Nacho said, before he went into the kitchen to help *Doña* Berta clear the dinner table.

Delia started up the stairs first. She glanced back and saw that María Elena had stopped to look at herself in the hall mirror.

Up in their room, Delia placed the typewriter case at the foot of her bed and the stack of paper on her desk. She took Juan Luis' gift, quickly wrapped it in her nightgown and locked the bathroom door behind her. She sat on the edge of the bathtub and her hands trembled when she untied the ribbon. Inside the golden foil, was a small book covered in soft burgundy leather inscribed in gold letters: *Los Hombres*, by Alberto Insúa.

She held the thin book in both hands as she were accepting a sacred offering. She read Juan Luis Rubio's handwriting on the endpaper: "*Con mi amor, para la que es mi vida.*" With my love, to the one who is my life. He had intertwined his initials at the end.

Delia brought the book up to her nose and breathed in the smell of new leather. In this moment, this instant, she forgot she was hiding in a bathroom, and felt that she could regulate the pulse in a young man's blood.

She began to turn the pages, thin as a butterfly's wings, and began to read the prologue. On the second page, Insúa had written:

The greatest thing in life and in the history of the spirit is repentance, that is, the act of lamenting sins incurred, with a firm commitment to rectification; the act of purifying, cleansing oneself, placing all confidence, not in the weak and limited individual, but in the infinity and magnitude of God . . . the God that belongs to all, who doesn't acknowledge privilege, aristocracies and democracies, but humility and virtue, from whose kindness and infinite beauty flow, like beams, the purest works of Intelligence and Art.

She closed the book and pressed it against her bosom. After changing into her nightgown, Delia folded the wrapping foil into a small square that fit inside the book, then hid the book itself inside her folded clothes. Slowly, Delia braided her hair using the ribbon that had held together Juan Luis Rubio's gift.

With every turn of the ribbon, she repeated the words he had written: "The one who is my life."

How romantic Juan Luis was! How fearless! He hadn't violated their parents' agreement because there was no letter involved; but he had reached her, and she wondered how many other ways he would find to express his love in the two or three years before they could be *novios*. Until then, she would settle for this delicious sense of shared guilt.

María Elena put the jewelry box on her dresser. She opened a top drawer, reached toward the back and brought out a small package.

Delia watched her sister unwrap a white box.

"Do I need to ask who gave you that present, Nena?"

María Elena held the contents in her fist, against her chest.

"I'll let you see it if you promise to keep quiet about it."

"Come on, just let me see it," Delia said, reaching for her sister's hand.

María Elena opened her fist. It held a small silver pin in the shape of a heart pierced with an arrow.

Delia lifted it from María Elena's hand and turned it over. She brought the pin closer to the light of a bureau lamp.

"It isn't inscribed."

"Of course not. Not yet. Remember, as far as Papá and Mamá are concerned, this pin doesn't exist."

María Elena took it from Delia and placed it back in its box. She hid the box in the back of a drawer, under some seldom-worn garments.

Delia muttered, "Is Mamá going to find another piece missing in her jewelry box?"

María Elena turned quickly, glared at her sister, then softened. She looked out the open bedroom door that let in the glow of the colored lights and the smell of fresh pine from the Christmas tree.

"Forget about it, won't you?"

"How can I? Every time Mamá reaches for her medallion and it isn't there, she blames me. She punished me, but that didn't end anything. She must wonder why I took it, what I did with it."

Delia sat on her bed and bent down to take off a slipper. María Elena placed her hand on Delia's shoulder.

"Has she said anything else to you about it?"

Delia looked up. "No. But that is not the sort of thing Mamá would forget. I don't either. Was he wearing it tonight?"

María Elena raised her hands up to her head in exasperation. "I'm not talking about this anymore! So don't bring it up again, understand?"

She turned toward the door at the sound of their parents' footsteps on the hallway. She waited until she heard their bedroom door being closed.

Delia waited, too. She knew well what would come next and decided to steal the wind from her sister's sail. "Would you still kill yourself with a knife? Or have you thought of something less messy?" Delia whispered.

Her sister's confusion gave Delia some pleasure. She chuckled and started to turn down her bed.

María Elena reached for Delia's arm and turned her around.

"I am not playing games, *hermanita*! You tell, I die. And I'll take with me our Mamá's joy!"

Delia shook off her sister's grasp.

"You don't scare me anymore, María Elena. I am going to sleep. ¡Feliz Navidad!"

María Elena didn't answer. She walked out to the balcony. The flashing lights of the Christmas tree gave her figure an ethereal quality that belied the burdens she carried.

Delia faced the mirror, brushed her hair with one hand, and held the back of the other hand against her cheek.

She could still feel the warmth of Juan Luis Rubio's touch. Under her pillow was the book he had given her.

Delia was still awake when her sister came back into the room, closing the door against the cool breeze that had started to rustle leaves and stir a potpourri of jasmine and honeysuckle.

Does she have any idea, Delia wondered, that she is Mamá's shame, not her joy?

Chapter 17

Once the holidays were over, the Pineda household again settled into a routine. The oppressive humidity called for frequent rest breaks and dinners were served later in the evening, when rainy afternoons gave way to cooler nights. The Pineda daughters prepared for final exams and made tentative plans for the new school term. With Carnaval coming in late February and Semana Santa following in early April, the start of the new term seemed far away. It would be María Elena's freshman year at the university and Delia's junior year in high school.

Juliana had returned from the interior with a bundle of sugar cane, baskets full of fruit preserves (including Delia's favorite, cashew marmalade), and blocks of ripe tamarind that she transformed into cooling beverages sweetened with raw brown sugar.

Delia and Josefita sat in the kitchen drinking *chicha de tamarindo* and discussed the merits of two shorthand methods they could choose to learn the coming school year.

"I think I'll stay with Pitman," Delia said, "that is what Mamá uses, and I can read her notes."

"But Pitman is a thing of the past," Josefita said. "Everyone uses Gregg now. It is easier."

She took a pencil from a cup and drew a fast loop on a lined tablet.

"Just like that. Easy to write, easy to read," Josefita Loma said and closed the tablet as if to end the discussion. "I didn't know your mother took shorthand."

"She was a court recorder a long time ago. She still writes notes to herself in shorthand if she is in a hurry."

The sound of María Elena's voice interrupted them.

"Juliana, where are the pieces of sugar cane I asked you to save for me?" she shouted from inside the *despensa*.

Cans and glass jars clinked on the shelves.
"I can't find anything in here, Juliana!"

146

Juliana reached for a towel and hurried into the *despensa*, wiping suds from her hands.

"They are outside, *niña*. If we keep them in here, the ants will come in. Look in the basket that *Doña* Berta keeps on the old table in the patio. The sugar cane is wrapped in plantain leaves. Just take what you need," Juliana said, ushering María Elena out the kitchen door.

"Watch out for ants and rewrap the rest," Juliana called after her.

She shook her head and grumbled when she walked back to the pantry and Delia heard her replacing the jars and cans María Elena had moved.

Josefita leaned closer to Delia and whispered, "You didn't tell me that Nena wants to run for Carnaval queen this year."

Delia pulled back. Then leaned towards Josefita.

"She does? Where did you hear that?"

"Isabel. It seems Nena and Alberto talked about it in front of Toñito, and he told his mother."

"She hasn't said anything here. I doubt that Papá would allow it. Besides, it is a bit late to enter the competition. The girls that are running for queen have already starting selling votes. She was probably teasing Alberto."

Josefita opened her mouth, as if to say something, but didn't.

"What is it, Josefita?"

"Oh, nothing . . ."

Delia elbowed her. "What were you going to say?"

"Daniela Morán is selling a lot of votes. She goes to the same school as María Elena and seems to have the lawyers behind her, with her father being a lawyer and all . . ."

The way Josefita looked at her unnerved Delia. She stood up, took their glasses to a counter and refilled their drinks.

So that was it. María Elena wanted to compete against her half-sister. Did they talk to each other, the lawyer's daughter by his wife and the lawyer's daughter by his lover? Also, did Josefita suspect, or worse yet, *know* of a connection between Nena and Daniela Morán? She needed to find out.

"Why did you bring up Daniela, Fita? There are others running too, no?

"Yes, but I've heard she's ahead on votes. I've also heard that your sister doesn't like her. The two of them have argued at school."

"What about?" Delia tried not to sound more than mildly curious, but she trembled inside. She reached for a dishtowel and wiped the kitchen counter, giving herself time to calm down.

"I don't know. But I heard it got nasty. A nun had to shut them up."

Delia let it go at that. Juliana had come back in the kitchen.

When Delia set the drinks on the table, she heard Papá's voice. "Too much sugar cane will get you dentures early in life," he said.

He was outside, helping Mamá weed the flower beds.

"I am not eating it. I promised Toñito I would help him catch *cocuyos* tonight and we need to make a house for them," María Elena said.

"Here, let me get that for you, Nena." Papá's voice sounded closer to the kitchen window.

Delia heard the blade of the knife scraping against the cane.

"I'll cut a door on this piece. Like this. You see? That'll fit back on snugly after you carve a space for bugs. Take some of this string to tie around the cut piece so it doesn't fall off."

"How many *cocuyos* can we get in there?" she asked.

"Enough to keep Toñito happy for a couple of days," Papá said.

"Catch those bugs soon after dusk and come home early, *hija*," Mamá said.

"I'll be back in time for dinner, Mamá." María Elena's voice trailed before the entry gate closed.

Inside, Josefita and Delia looked at each other. Delia knew what was on Josefita's mind: María Elena would have Alberto Guzman's company when she went to the mangrove trees near the bay to catch fire beetles with Toñito. With Juliana puttering around in the kitchen, the two friends refrained from further talk.

That evening, alone in their bedroom, Delia took her diary from the drawer of her bedside table, propped two pillows against the bed's headboard and leaned back against them.

She looked out the window on the moonless night when the topmost leaves of the mango tree only reflected the light from the streetlight. She heard Mamá's voice and María Elena's laughter. The hammock's hooks squeaked as Papá swung and she heard him whistling "Bésame Mucho."

Delia breathed deeply, taking in the ocean breeze mixed with the fragrance of the flowers from the ylang-ylang tree Papá had planted when she was born. She leaned forward and opened the diary. Only the first page had any writing on it:

> The loudest words are unsaid. The deepest feelings, smothered. Battles loom, without contenders. Wounds go untreated and fester as time passes. Will I have the courage to shout, to fight, to heal? And if so, when?

Delia had made the diary entry the day she knelt on dry corn. She leaned back against the headboard and threw the diary. It hit the wall and fell open, coming to rest upside down on the floor like a ballerina doing a split.

She picked up the book that Juan Luis had given her for Christmas from the bedside table, read a few paragraphs, then closed it and stared at the ceiling. Josefita's words had not left her: *The two of them have argued at school . . . It got nasty . . . A nun had to shut them up . . .*

What would it be like to have siblings living in another household with whom she shared nothing, not even a name? What was it like for María Elena, knowing she had two fathers, an adoptive father who loved her and provided for her, a real one who didn't even acknowledge her existence and gave his love to his other children.

Although she felt the choking grip of Mamá's secret, Delia couldn't help ruminating over the issue.

Is that why Nena wants to compete, why she quarreled with Daniela Morán? Does Daniela Morán know they share a father? Does María Elena sneak around with Alberto Guzmán because she wants to belong to that group of *rabiblancos* enough to risk her reputation?

The Guzmáns and the Moráns moved among the Country Club crowd the working mestizos had dubbed "whitetailed." Most of María Elena's school chums were legitimate daughters of *rabiblancos*.

On the other hand, Delia had begun to understand her sister's need to be with Alberto. She had started to feel the same need herself as time passed and Juan Luis Rubio continued to remind her, in subtle ways, that he loved her.

Juan Luis didn't show an interest in any other girl, and when he played his trumpet, its long, silky, vibrant sounds spoke to her, urged her to long for time to pass faster and bring them to the day when their love would come to full bloom.

So far her sister had no reason to report any misconduct from Delia to their parents. Delia had kept busy and avoided gossip by following Papá's orders; but upon their graduation from high school, Juan Luis would talk to Papá and ask permission to court her. Delia knew that when that day came, she would be ready to focus on Juan Luis.

When she imagined her future, he was in the picture. They still had more schooling ahead of them. But a *compromiso* did not mean a wedding was immediate. Delia knew of many couples who remained engaged for years. She liked that idea. Get to know each other well, plan together before they had children.

Abruptly, María Elena walked in wiping tears off her cheeks. Delia got up and sat on her sister's bed facing her.

"What's happened to you?"

"It's Papá. He is so *old-fashioned!*" María Elena kicked off one shoe, then the other. It landed against Delia's diary. "He won't let me try for Carnaval queen. He said no daughter of his is going to exhibit herself dancing on a float for four days and be gawked at by drunken rabble. He said I can only ride on a convertible to show off my *pollera* on Shrove Tuesday. You know he and Mamá will be in the car, too."

"Why do you want to be Carnaval queen? You'd have to go out and ask people to buy votes," Delia said. "It's too late to start that, anyway. There are others ahead of you . . ." She let the last sentence drift.

María Elena looked at her as if to pose a question, but instead brushed the back of her hand against her nose. "I'm as good as any of those girls running for queen," she cried.

You mean as good as your half-sister Daniela Morán, Delia thought. Oh, the demons she would unleash if she said it out loud, the hurt she could cause to Nena, to Mamá. She went on, attempting to calm her sister. "But I think asking people to buy votes for you is embarrassing. And Papá can't sponsor you himself. It costs too much money."

The Carnaval queen was chosen by the amount of votes she sold. Like it or not, it was a contest in which popularity and wealth played a major role. Invariably, the Carnaval queen came from among the *rabiblancos*.

"You would also need other costumes besides the *pollera* to wear the three days before Shrove Tuesday."

María Elena slapped the bed and shook her head in rejection.

"Oh, shut up, Delia. Just because no one would elect you for anything, you don't have to preach to me."

Delia stood up and picked up her diary.

"No one is preaching to you, Nena. And I am not running for anything. I don't need that. Just remember who is the one breathing through her mouth every night because her nose is pinched with pieces of cork. Was it Alberto's idea that you run for Carnaval queen?"

María Elena's late return from gathering *cocuyos* with Toñito had delayed dinnertime for nearly a half hour. When she finally came into the dining room, she looked like she had been running and Papá had given her a stern look. Now, when Delia mentioned Alberto Guzmán, María Elena turned her back on her sister and started another flood of tears.

Delia's compassion turned to anger. "Stop whimpering!" She lowered her voice. "Or you won't be able to hear Alberto's whistle when he comes to stand across the street to look up at our window."

Delia held up her hands when her sister gasped, stood up suddenly and came toward her.

"Don't worry. As far as I'm concerned, until Mamá and Papá catch on, and that may happen, you can go ahead trying to see each other at a distance. In the dark!"

Delia leaned her back against her dresser and held the diary against her chest. She wondered if some day she would want to run the risk to meet Juan Luis Rubio behind her parents' backs.

"Do you really enjoy that, Nena? When does Alberto plan to speak to Papá? Or isn't he serious enough about you?"

"Don't ask that," María Elena said, looking at the floor and sniffling. "It doesn't concern you. Stay out of this."

Delia pushed a little more. "What did Mamá say when you told them that you wanted to run for Carnaval queen?"

"She was for it. But you know how it is, Papá has the last word and he didn't even want to discuss it."

Delia put her diary back in the drawer and left the room.

The house was quiet. The only light downstairs came from the panel on the stove. Juliana had gone to her room. Mamá and Papá were gone. They often took late walks in the summer.

As Delia entered the kitchen, the wall clock in the *sala* rang the half hour past eleven.

Delia poured milk in a saucepan, turned on the stove and watched the liquid until steam began to rise from it. While she poured the warm milk in a cup, she wondered why confrontations with María Elena always left her thirsty. Of course Mamá would want Nena to compete against Daniela Morán, show off, triumph over Pablo Luis Morán's other daughter.

Delia unlocked the kitchen door and walked outside. She leaned against one of the posts under the second story balcony. She could smell the pungent ooze from green papayas that Juliana had scored with a knife and left outside to ripen.

A soft, distinctive whistle mingled with the yapping of the neighbor's dog.

Chapter 18

During school vacation Delia and María Elena were not expect-ed to wake up in time to have breakfast with their father, but Delia's night had been restless. She helped Juliana set the table.

"I hope *la niña* Nena doesn't make a habit of being late to din-ner. I thought *Don* Nacho would explode last night," Juliana said.

"It was the first time, Juliana," Delia remarked.

"That's how it starts. With the first time."

Delia touched Juliana's arm. "What are you trying to say?"

"Nothing, really. Nothing that would concern you. It's just that . . ." She hesitated. "She shouldn't make a habit of it."

Delia watched Juliana's hand shake when she poured freshly squeezed orange juice from a pitcher.

"Why?"

Juliana didn't answer.

"Why, Juliana, what makes you think it could become a habit?" she insisted.

The old woman set the pitcher on the counter and carried filled glasses to the table, talking without looking at Delia. "*Niña* Delia, girls do foolish things when they are growing up. Like your moth-er says, you don't want to give the neighbors reason to talk . . ."

"Are they talking?"

Juliana turned to face Delia and her hands flew to her face. "Oh, no, no, *niña* Delia!"

"What then? What are you worried about?"

Delia held Juliana's shoulders. She was taller now than the old woman and gaining a stronger sense of authority in their relation-ship.

Juliana's look shifted toward the door that connected the kitchen to the rest of the house.

"Your sister needs to give up this idea of running against Daniela Morán for Carnaval queen. She needs to leave that alone. It isn't good. It's embarrassing, shameful."

Delia let go of Juliana. Mamá and Papá were talking as they came down the stairs into the dining room.

She knows. She knows they are half-sisters.

Delia's vision blurred and a shrill sound reverberated in her ears. She walked out to the patio and took in several deep breaths to calm herself, then started yanking weeds from a flower bed with such force that she uprooted some seedlings.

After a few minutes, her hands muddied, Delia straightened up and went to wash her hands in the kitchen sink. She didn't speak to Juliana. Delia was a Pineda and the Pinedas kept their place, even when it came to sharing family secrets with a woman who had served them and shared their roof from as far back as Delia could remember. So what if Juliana knew about María Elena's birth? Delia would not lower herself to talking about it with her.

She went out again and circumvented the house, entering through another door to avoid her parents.

María Elena still slept. Delia felt a new surge of anger. Quietly, she changed into her swimsuit and pulled on a loose-fitting dress over it. She took a towel from the linen closet.

She stopped briefly at the dining room door.

"Mamá," she began. Unaccustomed to lying, she wasn't sure what to say. "I, I'm—"

"What happened to 'Good morning'?" Papá said, buttering a piece of corn tortilla.

"I'm sorry. Good morning Papá, Mamá. I'm going to the beach."

Mamá poured coffee. "Did you have breakfast, *niñas*?"

Delia tried not to stammer. "María Elena isn't coming. She's still sleeping. I'm stopping at Josefita's house. We won't stay long. I'll eat when I come back."

Delia started to walk away when her father called out, "You two watch out for the surf, the tide will be rising."

Delia didn't answer. She rushed past the gate and didn't slow down until she turned the corner. When she was sure she couldn't be seen by anyone at home, Delia stopped to catch her breath.

She felt worst than she did after her confrontations with María Elena. She had purposely lied to her parents and involved Josefita to boot.

And all because of Juliana. No. Because of Nena. No. Because of Mamá. No, not Mamá. Because of María Elena's father: Pablo Luis Morán. He was the one to blame. If he hadn't seduced Mamá, Nena would not have been born, she wouldn't be wanting to be Carnaval queen and Juliana would not have talked the way she did this morning. Delia draped the towel over her shoulders and wished lightning would strike Pablo Luis Morán. But she had heard Mamá tell Otilia once that every Christian had a cross to bear. Not being able to acknowledge it openly without causing shame and embarrassment to Mamá and María Elena, made Delia's cross heavier.

She stopped at Josefita Loma's house. She prayed her friend would still be sleeping. She needed to be alone to sort her thoughts and relieve the oppression she felt.

For the first time that day luck was on Delia's side and she left word with Josefita's mother that she would be waiting for Josefita at the beach.

"No need to rush," Delia said, "don't wake her. She can come to join me after she eats her breakfast."

Linda Vista beach was almost deserted at that hour save for two men hauling a fishing net into a boat and an old man with a boy digging around in the sand, collecting shells in a paper bag. Delia spread the towel on the sand and sat facing the water that shimmered, reflecting the early morning sun. She took off her sneakers and shook sand from them, then laid them next to her. She turned her face up and closed her eyes. The sun did not take away the inner chill that had first crept into her body when she had lied to her parents and now saturated every inch of her.

Not far from her, empty, stood the bench where she and Papá had sat to talk about Juan Luis Rubio's letter nearly a year ago. Things were different then. She could confide in her father about that event in her life; but the burden that weighed her down now had become heavier since that Easter Sunday when she had eavesdropped on her mother's chat with Otilia. She had come to that knowledge through devious means and bringing up what she knew would hurt Papá because Mamá was the source of her burden. It was Mamá's secret and Papa loved her, sins and all.

For the first time ever, Delia felt utterly alone. She wondered if her mother felt as desolate when she went to Otilia's home to have her bastard child, to hide the event if only for a while. And now, Mamá surely knew that all the years, and all Papá's love, couldn't erase people's memory. Not even Juliana's.

The surf started to break closer to her and a flock of seagulls screeched, circling above the fishermen. She stood up and stretched. Every muscle in her body felt knotted. She picked up the towel and the sneakers and placed them under the shade of a palm tree. She stripped down to her swimsuit and weighed down the dress with the shoes, then walked into the ocean past the breaking waves, and swam parallel to the shore. When her arms began to feel tired, she floated on her back, suspended on the cool water as if she were a baby in a cradle.

When she felt more relaxed, she paddled toward the beach. She watched the old man stumble, struggling to keep up with the boy who ran ahead of him, chasing the bubbles left by small clams burrowing in the sand. The fishermen had left the boat on the shore and now walked toward the bait shop beyond the palm grove. She turned her back on all that. She was glad that her only company would be the plovers and sandpipers that scavenged in the driftwood scattered along the beach and the seagulls that still circled above the boat.

She patted herself with the towel and squeezed salt water from her braid. She was tying the towel around her waist, when she heard the faint notes of a musical scale played on a trumpet and her heart skipped a beat. She picked up her dress and her sneakers and tried to reach the shady palm grove before Juan Luis Rubio could notice her from the distance.

He stopped playing. A moment later, she heard the familiar notes of the song he played for her coming closer.

Not this too, not today. And where was Josefita?

He ended the song holding a high note until she turned around to face him. He had started to turn red from the effort, his thick eyebrows arched, eyes were fixed on her. The wind blew his hair across his forehead. She felt the urge to touch, to smooth it back. She started to raise her hand, but stopped when he doubled over and puffed.

"Do you want to kill me? It's hard to hold a note that long!" he said, catching his breath.

She giggled. "What are you doing here?"

"Practicing. My mother and my sisters like it this way."

"Oh, come on," she said.

"I'm not kidding. They light candles to Saint Cecilia and pray to her to take me and my trumpet out of the house."

He leaned back and looked at her up and down. "What about you? I never saw you around here alone, this early." He looked at his watch. "It isn't even seven thirty yet."

Delia shrugged. "Josefita is supposed to meet me here, just to swim."

She added half a lie to her tally.

"I stopped at her house and left word for her to come to the beach." She looked around. "She should be here any minute."

"Even when you're wet, you're beautiful," he said, looking at the top of her breasts, which the swimsuit didn't cover.

She knew she was blushing when she sat under a palm tree. She couldn't put on her dress now. It would get wet and she still had to walk several blocks to go home. She had to let the swimsuit dry. She had to stay and wait for Josefita. And Juan Luis Rubio wasn't going away.

He sat on a piece of driftwood across from her, slipped off his leather sandals and rolled up his pant legs to the knees. He took off his shirt and wrapped the trumpet in it.

Watching him do this, when they were alone for the first time since their parents had talked about them, seemed so intimate a moment to Delia that it took her breath away. Juan Luis would be seventeen years old in another month and his naked torso showed strong muscles under a downy mat of black hairs.

Oh, God, what if someone saw them! Where was Josefita!

"Aren't you going to practice anymore?"

"Not right now. I'd rather talk to you. I can't miss this chance," he smiled.

"We're not supposed to be alone, Juan Luis."

"I'm not going to compromise you," he said standing up and moving the piece of driftwood a few inches away. "See? I'm not even close enough to touch you."

She straightened her back and leaned against the trunk of the palm. "Be sure you keep it that way," she commanded, looking around to be sure no one was watching.

"So," Juan Luis said leaning his elbows on his knees, "what do you have to say?"

"About what?"

"Anything. I just want to hear you talk."

The tide was near its high point now and the surf boomed. Juan Luis's black hair, blown by a strong breeze, looked wild. Delia surveyed his slightly tanned face. The dark eyes that narrowed as she looked at them, the straight nose like his father's, the mouth that smiled at her, and the dimples. He looked happy, open to whatever life offered him.

A gold crucifix hung from a chain around his neck. It brought to mind Mamá's medallion and Nena, and reminded Delia why she had come to the beach.

"Do you have secrets?"

"I don't think so," he said. "Should I?"

"I don't know, doesn't everyone, every family?"

He shook his head slowly. "Not in my family. My mother is Italian, remember? She talks all the time. She says everything that comes to her mind. There's no room inside her for secrets. Besides, she says that it's useless not to talk things out. That secrets are like balloons: They either shrivel up, or they burst." His fingers extended to show an explosion. "Either way, they stop being secrets."

Not mine, Delia thought. Mine keep getting larger.

"What are your secrets, beautiful Delia Pineda?"

She shrugged. "They're not my secrets."

"But you know them," he said, pointing at her.

"Well, yes."

"So, they aren't secrets anymore. If more than one person knows, that's it. They're out. Kiss them goodbye!" he said, blowing a kiss toward her.

She wished it were that easy. Two seagulls had started pecking at something on the wet sand and she watched them, feeling Juan Luis' eyes on her.

"Do you want to tell me those secrets?" he whispered.

Her mouth felt dry. "I can't." She licked her lips. They tasted salty.

"Then let's talk about us. Do you think about me? Do you dream about me?"

"Juan Luis!" She stood up, as if he had insulted her.

"Aha!" He stood up, too, laughing. "I knew it. You do. You don't fool me." He took a step closer and became serious.

"Someday, you'll share your secrets with me," he whispered, caressing her arm. "There'll be no need in our home for secrets, remember that."

There was that fire again, flowing from her feet to her face and she knew it wasn't the hot sand.

"Play the trumpet, Juan Luis, please."

She leaned against the palm tree. He reached for the bundled shirt, unwrapped the instrument and let the shirt fall over the piece of driftwood.

The shore birds took flight at the sound of the trumpet over the ocean's roar and she listened as he played "All The Things You Are," hitting some sour notes; but it didn't matter to Delia. She closed her eyes, feeling the need to touch him, the need for his embrace, and prayed for Josefita to show up soon.

When she opened her eyes again, Delia saw her friend in the distance, shading her eyes and waving a towel at them.

Juan Luis ended the song before Josefita reached them.

"I got a peek at heaven this morning," he said with a smile. "I'm looking forward to marrying you, Delia."

With her friend coming closer, she felt safer, lighthearted. "We'll see about that. Just don't rely on your music for a living," she teased.

He groaned and picked up his shirt and sandals. He bowed to her.

"I leave my wounded pride with you. You already have my heart. *Hasta pronto, mi amor*," he said and walked away, stopping briefly to talk to Josefita.

"Am I supposed to be chaperoning you?" Josefita Loma stood, arms akimbo, in front of Delia. "I rushed through my breakfast, wondering what we were supposed to be doing here this early, all of a sudden." Her tone softened and she pointed in Juan Luis' direction with her thumb. "*Oye*, Delia, how long have you been doing this?"

"I just had to get away from the house," Delia said. "Nena is pouting because Papá won't let her run for Carnaval queen."

Josefita nodded and rubbed her tongue along the inside of her cheek. "Uh-huh."

They watched Juan Luis walking away, his shirt thrown over his shoulder. "And what about him? Did you swim together? What did you talk about?" Josefita asked.

"Oh, stop it, Fita." Delia said undoing her braid. "We weren't alone that long. He got here just before you did."

"Is that why you're nervous?" Josefita smiled.

"Who's nervous?" Delia said running her fingers through her hair.

"You're fiddling with your hair. You always do that when you're nervous."

"Listen, Fita, he just showed up. He says he practices his music here often. I had no idea . . . We only talked."

"So that's it?"

"I just didn't want to be around to watch Nena sulking and you know we're not supposed to swim alone."

Josefita searched Delia's eyes for a moment. Then she pulled off her blouse and slipped off her skirt. "Then we better do what you said we came to do," Josefita sighed and ran towards the surf.

Following her, Delia felt the pressure go up another notch.

Chapter 19

Three weeks later, Delia sat looking out the open window of the bus she was taking to the city center. She reached back, lifted her hair, and leaned forward to let the warm breeze blow on her neck and back. Multicolored banners hung above the street on each block and intersection of Central Avenue, open invitations fluttering, enticing everyone to enjoy the carefree days of Carnaval.

The banners began at the once aristocratic colonial quarter near the Pacific shore, where multi-storied buildings with red tile roofs surrounded the Presidential Palace, and continued as far as the well-manicured Canal Zone. They ended just before reaching the rickety clapboard tenements clustered around *patios*. From a bird's-eye view, these formed a patchwork of empty lots piled with rubble, rusted corrugated roofs (that often blew away during hurricanes), and lines of laundry hung from balconies like flags of surrender. In these noisy enclaves, where several generations shared a room and multiple tenants shared one bathroom, Carnaval sprinkled its charm, too. From somewhere, as if by magic, Carnaval manifested itself in elaborate costumes and shiny musical instruments.

Delia saw tradition, wealth and hopelessness represented in the landscape of the city, all coming together for Carnaval, for a moment of abandon. The usual din, the stamp of life on crowded city streets, became more overwhelming with the sounds of cumbia, *tamborito*, rhumba, and samba that skipped over invisible social borders to wiggle their way into every corner of the city.

The sudden stops and starts of the bus made Delia a bit queasy. She tried to overcome the feeling by taking stock of other harbingers of Carnaval that hung over intersections: strings of colored lights arranged to form flowers and heavenly bodies; balconies displaying festive banners welcoming King Momo, blood cousin to Bacchus and ruler over the four days of music, parades, excessive drinking, and sensual indulgence that characterized the four days ending at dawn on Ash Wednesday.

161

How short those days seemed after the months spent in preparation. How quickly the glow vanished. If the adornments of Carnaval were left on the streets longer, would they continue to feed sad souls, would the gaiety linger? That was the reason for the passion, the wildness, Delia concluded, to grab joy at any cost before it slipped away.

With her index finger, she pulled the dirty cord above the window to ring the bell that signaled the bus driver to stop. She held her breath as she made her way out of the crowded bus redolent of human musk, cheap perfume and engine fumes.

Delia walked more than a block on a narrow side street to pick up Mamá's lottery tickets from a vendor. Mamá had regular numbers that she bought every week from the same vendor, and others that she picked after consulting with Otilia about dreams or events in their lives. Mamá had dieffenbachia plants with spotted leaves that Ana had taught her to read for digits, and Otilia had a dog-eared book that interpreted the meaning of their dreams and suggested the numbers to buy. Someday Mamá would hit "the big one" and buy a vacation house for them at Coronado Beach.

Delia smiled at the prospect. It wasn't a matter of if, but *when* Mamá hit "the big one." Like Papá said, reality is born in your mind's eye if you don't put blinders over it, so Mamá made her plans for *when*.

Two women were already waiting at the bus stop when Delia returned. They held canvas bags overflowing with groceries and exchanged gossip. One of the women spoke in Caribbean patois and wore a low-cut blouse that showed her sunbaked cleavage spotted with round, overlapping puffs of white powder. The other one kept tugging at an errant brassiere strap. The next bus to arrive had standing room only, and Delia chose to walk the eleven blocks back home.

She crossed the street near the Cathedral square to have a closer look at a store window displaying costumes and advertising flyers for the various *toldos* that had been erected throughout the city. The open air dance halls featured local and imported orchestras and admitted dancers for a fee. The largest flyer advertised the Sonora

Matancera, with Celia Cruz and Perez Prado's band coming to perform at the upscale Toldo Tropical.

This year Delia would be allowed to dance in a *toldo* for the first time, Mamá and Papá chaperoning. Delia bit the inside of her lower lip at the thought. So much for fun.

Another flyer in the window got her attention. It had a photograph of Daniela Morán, flashing a wide smile. Under the photo, it read: *Daniela, Reina del Carnaval de la Alegría.*

Delia pondered this.

"Carnaval of Happiness," Delia murmured. What an unimaginative name the Morán girl had given the celebration.

The eyes in the black-and-white photograph seemed light, and Delia concluded they must be hazel, like Nena's. Daniela's hair showed black, but her nose was flared; perhaps not as much as Nena's, but definitely similar. She wanted to find obvious flaws so she could hate the girl, but couldn't. Daniela Morán looked as charming in the flyer and she did in the photos that had appeared in the newspapers, the ones that she had seen Papá ignore and Mamá push down into the trash without comment. Delia wondered if María Elena had clipped any of them. She felt a pang of jealousy at the thought of María Elena wanting a closer connection to her other half-sister.

She walked a few more blocks and crossed the street, approaching the corner near Papá's printshop. Young men had congregated to try their *piropos* on young women.

Alberto Guzmán wasn't there. He had outgrown that bunch.

A couple of the boys turned toward the printshop when they saw her coming. Papá stood at the door, talking with a customer.

Such a disappointment. She had started to enjoy hearing some of the milder blandishments aimed at her. If the boys at the corner were machos-in-training, as Justo had said, she felt she had the right to be a vamp-in-training.

Knowing she could get away with it this time, Delia slowed down, looked at each boy in the eye and smiled, adding a sway to her hips as she walked by them. She felt the wind blowing wisps of her hair.

I got it right, she thought.

"*Hola, chicos,*" she teased, her voice barely audible, knowing that Papá's presence nearby forced the boys to hold back.

"*Con permiso,*" Delia said, walking into the shop past Papá and the other man. Justo was on the phone and waved to her when he saw her.

Delia took a Coca-Cola from the small refrigerator her father kept in the back room, pried the cap with the bottle opener mounted on the wall, and went to sit at the window. Justo joined her soon after.

"What brings you here today, *chiquilla?*" he said. "We don't see much of you around here anymore."

"I'm busy."

"Doing what?"

"We had finals at school. I had to do some cramming."

"Let me guess." He stroked his chin and looked toward the ceiling. "Delia Pineda had to get a decent grade in math or she doesn't get to dance in a *toldo* this year."

"That wasn't a guess. Papá tells you too much." Delia took a sip from her Coca-Cola.

Papá stuck his head in the door and called to them, "I'll be back after a while. Pedro is buying me coffee."

They watched him walk away with his customer.

"Are you ready for Carnaval?" Justo asked, leaning on the windowsill.

"As ready as I'm going to be."

She looked toward the boys standing on the street corner.

"The guard is changing, Justo."

"Yes, you noticed. They make me feel old. Although it's only the faces that change. The *piropos* remain the same. In my youth, we thought we had a great deal of imagination."

"Did you stand on the corner, too?"

"No. My guard sat on a bench outside the grocery store owned by old Chang Li in Guararé. At fourteen, I was working in the fields cutting cane during the day and spent the evenings playing dominoes with my pals at old Chang Li's storefront, smoking Lucky Strikes, and chugging *cervezas.*"

"What about school?"

"That ended when I finished the sixth grade. After that, life was my school. A tough one, too."

"But you know so much about books, about the poets . . ." She placed the empty Coke bottle on a table behind her.

"I said life is a tough school, Delia." Justo lowered his voice. "For ten years I had little distractions and a deep wound to heal. I found that healing in the old books in the prison library. There weren't many, so I read the same books until I could almost repeat them word for word."

"I'm sorry, Justo."

"We all have a destiny. That was mine," Justo said, patting Delia's hand.

A man walked by the window. Over his shoulder, he carried hangers with several colorful costumes. Their eyes followed him until he walked into an alley from which came the rhythmic sound of hands slapping the tight skin of a conga drum.

"I see Daniela Morán's picture everywhere," Delia said, testing Justo.

His expression didn't change. He said, "She picked Alberto Guzmán to be her escort."

Delia turned to him, surprised.

"Really?"

"Isabel heard it on the radio when Daniela Morán was announcing the members of her court."

María Elena had to know about this, there must have been talk about it among her friends. It puzzled Delia that María Elena had shown no reaction to the news.

"Funny," Justo said shaking his head, "There was a time when I would've bet Alberto Guzmán would become María Elena's *novio*."

"Did you ever talk about them with Papá?"

"There was no need. Nena is not one to become involved with a young man without your parent's knowledge. Besides, of late, they seem to be going their own way. Not as friendly as they used to be."

That's what you think, Delia wanted to say. They're only more cautious now, because they have become closer. The adults around the Pineda daughters seemed so trusting of María Elena. Even Justo, whom she considered more perceptive than most, believed in Nena's candor. She felt a twinge of disappointment. She wondered if Justo could be counted among those who would set up María Elena as an example for her. If so, then loving and trusting a woman, and going to prison for her deceit, hadn't opened his eyes enough.

"Is he Daniela's *novio*?"

"I doubt it," Justo said. "He seems too involved in politics with the *universitarios* these days to give much attention to the *señoritas*. His father says that Alberto will be groomed to become president some day."

"A family tradition, I guess," she said. "His grandfather was president once."

"Only briefly, though. The Americans in the Canal Zone didn't like it too much when he sang the praises of Hitler."

Politics didn't interest Delia at this point. She wanted to get home and find out how María Elena was reacting to this new development.

"I've got to run, Justo. Mamá expected me to return home by bus and I walked instead. I'll see you later."

"I'll phone Berta and let her know you're on your way."

Delia still smarted from his comment about María Elena's trustworthiness. She turned around at the door.

"Justo, what is it about people that makes them cover their eyes and shut out the truth? Do you ever peek between your fingers?"

He picked up a rag and wiped his hands. "Sometimes the truth hurts, *chiquilla*. It isn't that we don't see it. It hurts less to ignore it. Sometimes we want to protect our loved ones."

"With lies?"

"With silence."

"I don't like it," Delia said and walked out, away from the boys standing on the street corner, away from the sound of the conga drum echoing in her chest.

Delia found Juliana in the kitchen wearing a twisted white cotton rag around her head to absorb her copious perspiration. She looked tired as she ironed the many yards of fine handworked linen that formed *Doña* Berta's *pollera*.

Delia poured a glass of ice water for each of them while Juliana hung up Mamá's dress.

"Is María Elena here?" Delia said, taking the lottery tickets from her purse.

"She's upstairs. Her *siesta* seems to last longer than everyone else's." Juliana's impatience came through her tone.

Delia placed the lottery tickets under the pot that held the dieffenbachia plant. Mamá kept them there for good luck. She started to leave the kitchen, but Juliana stopped her.

"I can use your help," she said, and gave Delia a ball of yarn. She reached for a blouse that hung from the door and placed it on the table. "Please finish your blouse for me. I still have a lot to do here before I can start to cook dinner."

Delia sat down and began to thread red yarn through the lace neckline of her *montuna* blouse. She would wear the less elaborate costume this year and the next, before she could ride in a convertible like Mamá and María Elena, displaying the delicate handwork and the costly jewels of the luxurious national dress.

Juliana wiped sweat off her neck with a towel and grumbled, "I should have stayed in the interior for another two months. Then *Doña* Berta would have hired someone else to iron all this mess!"

"And you would have missed Carnaval in the city," Delia smiled. "In the interior you would have been dancing in the street and getting soaked with water balloons. I'd rather be hit with confetti and serpentine streamers."

Juliana pointed at herself. "Me dancing on the streets? It's more likely I would be trampled. Carnaval is not for old women. We don't have anything left to shake."

She finished ironing Delia's red calico skirt and pinched its waist to a wire hanger with wooden clothespins.

"Are you riding in the car with *Doña* Berta on Tuesday?"

"Yes," Delia said, "but in front, with Papá. There isn't enough room in back once you spread out the skirts of two *polleras*. Isabel's in mourning, so she and Justo are staying home. Otherwise, I would ride with them in another car."

Delia tied two ends of yarn with a knot and attached red pompoms in the center front and back of the blouse. She smoothed out the folds on the neckline ruffle and hung it over the skirt and petticoat. She was in a hurry to finish here. She needed to talk to María Elena.

"So you won't be in a *comparsa*," Juliana said. She stood at the door and cooled herself with a fan of woven palm fronds.

"Papá wouldn't hear of it. María Elena never did, so I won't either. Like Mamá said, 'What your sister has never done, you want to do!'" Delia had *Doña* Berta's tone down pat.

Juliana pouted and shook her head. "Your time will come, *niña*."

"I see nothing wrong with a *comparsa*. Josefita has been meeting with around twenty of our friends. They have rehearsed their songs and line dances and they hired musicians. They have a different costume for every day of Carnaval and may win a prize. But I have to be content with watching from our balcony as they go by."

"Well, *niña* Delia, sometimes things can get out of hand with young people in the dancing groups. Many a girl has ended up blotting bitter tears a few months after Carnaval. With the dancing and the music and the liquor that the young men sneak around, comes trouble of the worst kind."

Delia watched Juliana as she picked a bundle from the straw basket that sat on the floor under the ironing board and unrolled the damp garment.

Juliana began to press the collar of Papá's *montuno* suit. Mamá had worked for several months counting threads to cross-stitch the various designs on the collar, the sleeves, around the front placket, and the more elaborate cockfight that covered most of the back.

Delia and María Elena had pulled the threads on the edges of the sleeves and of the legs of the calf-length breeches, to form a three-inch fringe. It flipped around as Papá walked and danced in *cutarras*, the rustic leather sandals made by the cobbler two doors from *Don* Nacho's printshop.

The sound of drums, blaring trumpets, and young people singing came closer and Delia walked out to the gate.

Doña Berta and María Elena were already there, watching one of the first organized dance groups that started the celebration on this afternoon of Sábado de Carnaval.

Elbows locked together, the group danced to and fro to the beat of the drums. Cars pulled over along the sidewalk to let them pass.

The dancers did not wear masks, but they were a high-spirited bunch of red satin devils. The young men, Juan Luis Rubio among them, carried black tridents. Some of the girls had wrapped the long tails of their costumes provocatively around their necks.

In the midst of them, Josefita Loma's face glowed. She let go of the arm of one of her dancing partners to wave in response to the Pineda's applause.

Behind Josefita's chorus followed a variety of traditional *diablillos*, wearing terrifying *papier-mâché* masks topped with long bird fathers. When *Doña* Berta threw coins for them, they scrambled to the pavement while drivers honked their car horns to make them move faster.

María Elena remained at the gate when Delia and *Doña* Berta began to walk back to the house.

"You see, Mamá, there are mostly kids from our school in Josefita's group. I wish you and Papá had let me join them. You even applauded them," Delia said.

"Let's not talk about it anymore. Nena never joined a group of dancers for Carnaval either and you don't see her complaining."

Delia had seen photos of her mother standing among a group of women dressed as Martinicans, her plaid turban topped with a knot that resembled a bird in flight.

"Did you ever dance in a *comparsa*, Mamá?"

"I did. But those were different times. Things change, *hija*."

Mamá turned around and waited for María Elena to catch up with them.

María Elena stepped between the two of them and entered the house first. She turned and put her arms around *Doña* Berta.

"I can't wait until Tuesday! I just can't wait to show off my *pollera*. People are going to applaud as we go by. Aren't they, Mamá?"

"*Sí, hija*, they will. But for now, you and Delia take some chairs out to the balcony."

Delia and María Elena took chairs from the bedrooms and lined them up along the elaborate wrought iron railing, for family and friends to sit and watch the first parade of floats later that day.

With the last chair in place, María Elena sat down, placed her arms on the railing, leaned her chin on them, and looked in the direction from which the parade would come.

Delia leaned against the balcony, facing her sister, her back toward the street.

"Are you going to stay here and wait for the queen's float? Are you looking forward to seeing Alberto escorting Daniela Morán?"

Escorting your sister, she wanted to say.

When María Elena turned and looked at Delia, the sadness in her eyes betrayed her.

"This is temporary. She begged him to escort her. After Shrove Tuesday, Alberto will have nothing else to do with Daniela."

"How do you know that?"

"He told me so. He promised me this meant nothing to him."

"Do you really believe that, or are you trying to convince yourself?"

María Elena stood up.

"Stop speculating. You can't understand these things. Not until you grow up. Besides, it has nothing to do with you."

María Elena took a step to go inside the house, but Delia put her hands firmly on her sister's arms, and lowered her voice.

"But it has something to do with me! What am I going to do if Mamá comes into our room at one in the morning and you are not there?"

María Elena's eyes grew wider as her face lost its color.

"You've been spying on me," she whispered. She freed her arms from her sister's grasp. "You jealous little worm. Just remember: If you love Mamá, you better keep your mouth shut."

Delia closed her eyes and swallowed hard. She heard the door slam.

Chapter 20

On the days that followed, the Pinedas hosted friends and watched the increasing revelry of Carnaval from their home. The various crews paraded in huge headdresses of multicolored feathers and costumes of sequins, silks, taffeta, even gossamer wings. They danced on the street uninhibited, carried away by the pulsing music, or they rode in floats that Delia saw as fantastic or nightmarish.

She watched her sister as the queen's float went by, expecting to see some strong reaction to Daniela Morán being in a place María Elena coveted, or perhaps a telling look from Alberto Guzmán.

But Alberto never looked their way, and María Elena simply didn't applaud as the float passed.

Mamá looked down at the Carnaval queen with disdain, and commented to Otilia that Nena would have been more regal.

Now, on Shrove Tuesday, the Pinedas prepared to join the last parade of cars and floats that bid good-bye to Carnaval.

"This will be the last year you'll wear your own hair this way for Carnaval," Mamá said, as she finished plaiting Delia's tresses with ribbons. She brought the braids forward to rest over her daughter's breasts.

Delia, on a stool facing Mamá's dressing table, straightened her *trenzas* and looked at herself in the mirror.

"I can't wait to get my hair cut short. I'm always the last one in our class to be in style. I wish Papá wasn't so adamant about keeping my hair long until I'm seventeen."

"Well, just go along with it, *hija*. You know he's strict. He thinks of a lady's hair as her crowning glory."

"And, don't forget, 'a man's perdition,' as he used to say about Isabel's hair."

Mother and daughter laughed.

Lately, when María Elena wasn't in the same room, Delia had started to feel a closer kinship with her mother. These were moments served to her like measured teaspoons of a delectable pudding for which only Mamá had the recipe.

Doña Berta stood behind Delia, and their image in the mirror made them both smile.

The perfect oval of Delia's face, her slightly upturned nose, matched her mother's. Her almond-shaped eyes, with irises the color of espresso coffee, duplicated *Doña* Berta Pineda's.

Delia liked to think that Mamá had saved her good looks to pass on to her.

"I hope to grow up to be as beautiful as you are, Mamá," Delia said, and swallowed the lump in her throat.

In the mirror she saw her mother's delicate hands resting gently on her shoulders. As a child, she had felt the sting of those hands on her cheeks; she knew that under the layer of decorum lived a mercurial woman.

Mamá leaned over and kissed the top of Delia's head.

"You're beautiful already, *hija*. Now, go on," she said, helping Delia up from the stool. "Ask Nena and Juliana to come in."

Juliana would help *Doña* Berta and María Elena attach braided hair extensions to their own short hair to support the ornate hairpins that trembled with every movement. Then she would add a jeweled comb to each side of their heads. Each comb had a curved end that pressed against the temple and called attention to the eyes.

Delia's love for Mamá was becoming less conditional. She felt an increasing awareness of her mother's feelings of betrayal by a man she had loved, the need to protect the fruit of that passion, and the need to shield her daughters from the kind of temptation that had caused her so much pain. Mamá's refusal to acknowledge that she wasn't the only source of information for her daughters, however, still seemed foolish to Delia.

She wrestled with her emotions. She never questioned the depth of her love for her father; but there had been times when her resentment toward her mother had been strong enough to stir guilt in her. But, knowing now the risks María Elena took, and cognizant of her own feelings, Delia forgave her mother. All this had changed

Delia; but it didn't change her Mamá. What would she do if she found out that Delia had been keeping María Elena's secrets?

Delia joined Papá, who waited in the *sala*, already wearing his *montuno* suit. He had grown a mustache for the occasion and had traded his usual cigarette for a burlwood pipe. The fine woven straw hat that completed his outfit hung from a rack near the front door.

"Handsome as always!" Delia said.

"That's nice to hear. Let me look at you, *querida*."

Don Nacho stood up, held his daughter's hands, and twirled her around.

"*¡Lindísima!* How about a *danzón*? I need to practice," he said.

Don Nacho ran his finger along a stack of records on a shelf and selected one. Soon music filled the room and he extended his arms inviting Delia to dance. She gathered the hem of her long skirt on one hand. When she raised her hand to *Don* Nacho's shoulder, a red calico fan surrounded them.

"You don't need to practice, Papá. You and Mamá will put the other dancers to shame. Are you staying out 'til dawn?"

"Of course, *querida*. The Pinedas don't break with tradition. When you see us tomorrow morning, we'll be ready to start the Cuaresma."

The blue Chevrolet convertible that carried the Pinedas stopped for a moment in the slow-moving traffic. They were surrounded by shouting and singing, music from live combos, and strident car horns, mixed with the shouts of vendors selling balloons, drinks, and food. As Papá drove, the Pinedas had to yell at each other to be heard. Confetti and serpentine streamers covered them and formed a thick carpet on the seats and floor of the convertible.

The Pinedas smiled, waved, and acknowledged the compliments of the parade watchers who crowded the sidewalks, windows and balconies. An off-duty policeman walked alongside the car, a precaution taken by Papá because *Doña* Berta and María Elena wore enough gold and pearls to tempt thugs.

On their way to take their position in the parade, the Pinedas passed the queen's float. At that moment, Alberto Guzmán helped Daniela Morán to her seat on the ornate platform. With one arm around her waist, he whispered in her ear.

Delia immediately looked at María Elena for a reaction; but the intense rancor in her sister's eyes wasn't directed at Alberto or Daniela. Nena's look was for a tall man going up to the platform. He appeared to be older than Papá because his dark brown hair had touches of gray. There was no question left in Delia's mind who had fathered María Elena and Daniela Morán. Pablo Luis Morán wasn't good-looking. But he did have the distinguished look that money, breeding, and confidence give. He fussed over his daughter and spoke to Alberto, who nodded in agreement.

Delia saw Mamá glance at the man for an instant, then reach over and squeeze one of María Elena's hands.

María Elena lowered her eyes and turned her back on the queen's float.

Delia ached for her sister and her sorrow deepened when María Elena and Mamá, no longer smiling, resumed waving to onlookers. Papá's whole attention was on steering the vehicle, following directions from a parade official. When Delia looked back, her mother signaled with her hand for her to turn around.

On foot, ahead of them, a samba school from Brazil brought to life the meaning of Carnaval. Their musicians beat drums with a frenzy. Tall, sun-bronzed women in high heels and lots of feathers on their heads and little else, shook generous breasts, shimmied bare buttocks, and thrust their pelvises in ecstasy, as if possessed by King Momo himself.

Under different circumstances, Mamá would have been terribly mortified by what she considered a shameful display of immorality. Giving in to the devil, submitting to the flesh, was Mamá's definition of samba dancing.

Letting down your hair before submitting to the severity of Lent, Papá called it. This was Carnaval and such behavior was part of it.

Delia watched the dancers and wondered what it would feel like to be that uninhibited, to display your body in public, moving it, letting the music drive you, inciting whistles and arousing others to obscene behavior.

A blurred shape leaped from the crowd.

Mamá screamed, Papá stepped on the brake and everyone lurched forward.

Delia turned around, and saw the hired policeman rushing from behind the car and wrestling a man. The crowd around them stepped back when the policeman pressed his knee to the back of a man wearing a loincloth. His body was completely covered with tattoos and his face had been painted to look like a tiger's.

The policeman held back one of the man's arms, tattooed so that a large snake seemed to encircle it. On his free elbow, a spider web contorted and a black spider expanded and contracted with the man's movements.

"*Ya, ya!*" the man screamed. "Let me go!"

Papá got out the car and bent over to see the man.

"He tried to touch *Doña* Berta's hand," the policeman said.

"Why?" Papá asked the man, looking closely at his painted face.

"I just wanted to tell her how beautiful she looks, I swear! I wasn't going to harm her," he whined.

"Just stay away, you hear?" Papá said angrily, and nodded to the policeman to let the man go.

"*¡Disimulen, niñas, disimulen!*" Mamá said behind clenched teeth. Delia raised her eyes and saw her mother and her sister spreading out their skirts with trembling hands. Their pallor betrayed their fear. She knew her own fear almost paralyzed her.

"Stay closer to the car," Papá said to the hired policeman, putting the car in gear. "Don't let it happen again!"

As they moved slowly forward, Delia watched Mamá and María Elena coolly resume their regal wave, smiling, while the sounds of Carnaval slowly seeped back into Delia's consciousness. It astonished Delia that they were so good at dissembling.

Delia's heart still raced, her hands felt icy. Did theirs?

A scarlet sunset washed over the city when the float parade ended and the Pinedas returned home. Outside, the hubbub of Carnaval continued. Revelers would pack the streets and dance halls until dawn, when they would dance their way to the seashore to bury sardines in the sand. The traditional ceremony symbolized the end of unrestrained carnality and the beginning of the fasting, sobriety, and self-scrutiny that came with Lent. The dawn of Ash Wednesday would find many of them still in costume, going home from early Mass, where the priest had thumbed a cross of ashes on their foreheads.

Delia and María Elena stood in the kitchen, shaking confetti from their hair and their clothes, laughing and pulling serpentine streamers off each other.

"So what's the program for tonight, *niñas*?" Juliana stirred a pot on the stove, dipped a wooden spoon in it, blew, and tasted the thick sauce before she covered the pot.

"Papá said we can go dancing at the *toldo* Tropical until midnight," Delia said, lifting the lid on the pot and breathing in the aroma of well-seasoned beef and vegetables.

"Just like Cinderella!" María Elena added.

Delia whispered in her sister's ear, "Not quite. Your prince will be dancing with the queen, remember?"

María Elena's smile made Delia's blood run cold.

"You should have been there, Juliana, a man tried to touch Mamá today at the parade," María Elena said.

Juliana's eyes opened wide.

"Really? What did *Don* Nacho do?"

"He let the man go," María Elena said.

"You sound disappointed," Delia said.

"Well, it was exciting! But they should have hauled that guy to jail! You should have seen him, Juliana, he had tattoos all over him!" María Elena gestured, moving her hands along her body.

"That was Emilio," Juliana nodded. "He's sort of an idiot. Got his tattoos when he went away with the Merchant Marine. Got into a nasty bar fight once and he hasn't been right in his head since. He's really harmless."

"I never saw him before," Delia said.

"You wouldn't, *niña*. He lives in Chorrera and only comes to the city at Carnaval time. He knows he has a ready-made costume with all those tattoos."

"That's about all he was wearing, too," María Elena said. "I saw his *nalgas*!" She slapped her buttocks.

Delia wasn't amused. "For someone as afraid as you were, you sure saw a lot."

That night, María Elena danced, but not with Alberto Guzmán. As escort to Daniela Morán, he was dancing at the Country Club.

Delia danced with several young men, among them Juan Luis Rubio. He made sure that they stayed within sight of Delia's parents, but that didn't prevent him from squeezing her hand to the lyrics of a romantic bolero. Delia felt delicate parts of her body swelling when he pressed his hand against the small of her back.

"Let's not dance for a while," he whispered once. "I feel you melting in my arms and that's dangerous, sweet Delia . . ."

Is that so? she thought. What about what you're feeling? Don't you think I know what's keeping you from holding me close?

A few minutes past midnight, *Don* Nacho brought his daughters home from the dance. Mamá waited for him at the *toldo* with Otilia and other friends.

Chapter 21

It took the sisters nearly an hour to unwind. María Elena had fallen silent first. After a while, Delia had relaxed enough to sleep.

When the clock in the *sala* rang half past four, Delia restlessly stirred, rolled over, and rubbed her eyes. Dim light from a nearby lamppost fell on María Elena's bed. It was empty.

She found the bathroom dark, its door ajar. When she was finished, Delia's curiosity took her to the *sala*, then the kitchen. There was no sign of María Elena. Delia found the kitchen door to the patio unlocked and she felt her stomach knotting.

From a *toldo* some blocks away came the fading sounds of drunken voices, laughter, the driving rhythm of cumbia. Someone passing in a car yelled *"¡Viva el Carnaval!"* and threw a bottle against the concrete wall. The frantic bark of the neighbor's dog mixed with the sound of glass shattering on the pavement.

A cold wave rose from Delia's feet and blood began to pump fast and loud inside her. It seemed to well behind her eyes and push them out, blurring her vision. Her short, light blue nightgown stuck to her clammy skin. She ran cold water over a dishtowel and held it against her forehead and her cheeks, breathing deeply until she felt calmer. Her hand trembled when she picked up a glass from a shelf, turned on the water faucet and quietly filled it.

Delia pulled out a chair and sat at the kitchen table. She stared at the carved wood napkin holder and matching salt and pepper shakers, Heinz ketchup bottle, slim Tabasco bottle, and the glass container of toothpicks gathered atop a lazy Susan. She surveyed the counter where a wooden block held sharp kitchen knives. Her pulse beat against her eardrums and she felt drops of perspiration on her forehead.

She reached for a napkin and overturned the toothpicks. *"¡Coño!"*

She shuddered when she heard herself utter the crude curse for the first time in her life. Oh, God, Father almighty! Forgive me! *¡Ave María Purísima!* Help me! I am going crazy . . .

She gathered the toothpicks, put them back in the container, and kept one. Shaking, she scraped the sharp end under her short fingernails, watching the white on the outgrowth. Her temples still throbbed and she wanted to close her eyes. Instead, she fixed them on the unlocked door.

The click of the back gate outside brought Delia back. Dawn had started to filter through the kitchen door's louvers. The pile of splintered toothpicks on the table startled her. She didn't remember snapping each one into tiny pieces. Not a single one remained whole in the container.

María Elena gasped, her hand flying to her mouth, when she came in and found her sister waiting by the kitchen counter. María Elena's blouse, usually tucked into her skirt, hung loose. Her face was red and swollen. María Elena's voice sounded heavy, her chest rising and falling as she tried to take in air: "What are you doing here?"

"Waiting for you. It's nearly daylight, Nena! Are you *crazy?* Have you been with Alberto all this time?"

"No." María Elena shook her head from side to side. An incredulous tone crept into her voice. "He didn't show up. I waited for hours. And he didn't show up."

María Elena abruptly squared her shoulders, wiped her eyes and confronted Delia. The old flame of daring had returned, but this time Delia saw a flicker of fear, not arrogance, on her sister's face.

María Elena started to leave the kitchen. "Let's go to bed. This isn't your problem."

Delia's knees weakened. She felt the walls pressing toward her from all sides.

"Yes. It is my problem now. I know about it and I want out."

María Elena turned. "You want out? What does that mean?"

Was this what Justo had meant when he talked about a thundering herd coming at you?

Delia felt herself spiraling in the vortex that had sucked in María Elena and she was in it for the ride. Gratis.

Here it goes. *O corres, o te encaramas.* Yes, either you run or you get on with it.

"I'm telling Papá and Mamá about this." Her voice trembled and squeaked. So what!

María Elena looked around, desperate, searching.

Delia swallowed hard and when she spoke, her voice was clear, firm, disguising the fear that invaded every cell of her body.

"Here! Go ahead. Do it!" she said, thrusting a sharp, long kitchen knife that she'd held behind her back toward María Elena.

María Elena wasn't looking at the knife. She stared at Delia, incredulous.

"*¿Anda, qué esperas?*" Delia said, thrusting the knife forward again. "Can't you keep a promise, Nena? I said I am telling. Now, what are you waiting for? Kill yourself!"

She lifted María Elena's hand and slapped the wooden handle into her palm, cutting her own hand as she gave the knife to her sister.

María Elena looked at the knife in her hand, its blade glinting. Trembling, she wrapped the palm of her other hand on the knife's handle and, with a shaking, two-handed grip, slowly pointed the blade toward her stomach. Her eyes pleaded and tears streamed down her pale, horror-stricken face.

Delia didn't flinch. She pressed her lips together hard. It felt good. She had the sensation of ugly, dead layers of skin peeling away, falling to the floor, and resting around her in a mound. All she had to do was step over it and she would feel lighter. She could levitate if she wanted to.

"What's stopping you. Need help?" She reached toward María Elena. She could feel the cut on her hand, now, and blood stained her nightgown.

María Elena fell to her knees, convulsed and dropped the knife.

Delia kicked it hard and saw it slide on the polished tile floor and stop at Papá's feet.

Papá! How long had he been standing there?

Now Mamá came into focus, too. They had come in through the front door and must have heard the voices in the kitchen. Still wearing their Carnaval costumes, their real selves masked, they didn't belong in the picture.

Delia felt the vertigo of standing at the edge of a deep chasm, with Papá and Mamá poised on the opposite side.

Papá picked up the knife and set it on the counter and Mamá rushed to help María Elena to a chair.

María Elena wept and moaned. "Oh, no, Delia, Don't . . ."

Papá's voice sounded like thunder, cutting through the ringing in Delia's ears.

"What is going on here!"

"Shh, shh, Nacho, you'll wake up Juliana," Mamá pleaded.

"¡Me importa un carajo! I don't care if the whole neighborhood wakes up!"

He came to stand in front of Delia.

"What is all this, Delia?"

O corres o te encaramas. No more bluffing. It was time to free herself.

Delia leaned against the kitchen counter. She felt her knees about to buckle. She turned on the faucet and let water run over her cut hand. She didn't want to look at her father.

Juliana stood at the door, her eyes big as a frightened doe's, one hand over her mouth and the other holding her robe together over her nightgown.

"María Elena has something to tell you. She just came in," Delia said, wrapping a clean kitchen towel around her hand. If only she could bandage her Papá's heart in the same way! She turned toward him.

Don Nacho had turned pale. He squeezed his eyes shut for a moment and then spun around to face María Elena.

"You went out tonight? Alone? Like a whore?" He raised his hand as if to strike her. At the same time, Mamá let go of María Elena and clutched her hands to her chest.

Don Nacho stopped in mid-motion and caught *Doña* Berta in his arms. He could hardly hang on to her limp body. He bumped the table and the lazy Susan fell to the floor, bottles and napkins scattering everywhere.

"Juliana, get the ammonia!" Delia yelled.

She helped *Don* Nacho steady *Doña* Berta in a chair, while Juliana held the ammonia bottle near *Doña* Berta's nose.

When Mamá reacted, she nearly knocked the bottle from Juliana's hands.

María Elena stood up.

"You're going to kill her!" she shouted at Delia.

Don Nacho grasped María Elena's arm and turned her toward him.

"Where were you, Nena, and who were you with?"

María Elena shook off *Don* Nacho's grip, turned around and slapped Delia.

"You are no longer my sister!"

Delia's cheek stung, but she didn't move.

"I will always be your sister," she sighed. "Like Daniela Morán is your sister." Then came the warning, so many years overdue, "And don't ever hit me again. You can't bully me any more."

Mamá covered her face with her hands, smudging the ashes on her forehead.

"No, no, Nacho, did you tell her?" she moaned.

Papá didn't respond. He kept looking at Delia. She saw understanding in his eyes. The ashes on his forehead were intact. She could see the imprint of the priest's thumb.

"She can also tell you who is wearing Mamá's medallion," Delia told him. Tears welled in her eyes. He opened his arms and she fell into them, sobbing.

"It's over, *querida*, it's all over . . . I'm so sorry. We should have told you," Papá said.

Mamá stood up suddenly and faced María Elena.

"Have you been with a man?"

María Elena lowered her eyes.

Mamá began hitting her oldest daughter with her fists. María Elena raised her arms to deflect the blows, all the time crying, "No, Mamá, *no me pegue!*"

Don Nacho let go of Delia and restrained his wife.

"Nena will have to get married, Nacho." Mamá seemed dazed.

"No, that's not the way. He doesn't love her or he would have talked to us." He turned to María Elena. "We trusted you."

"But she's no longer a *señorita*, she's disgraced us!" Mamá said.

"*Ya basta*, Berta!" Papá said, holding up his hands. "That's enough! No more lies, no more secrets."

María Elena ran upstairs.

Juliana sat Delia at the table and began to bandage her hand. Papá slowly helped Mamá up the stairs, calming her as they went. Delia heard their footsteps as they entered their daughters' bedroom.

"Stay here, *niña* Delia. Let them deal with it," Juliana said, gathering the bottles and the lazy Susan from the floor.

Juliana swept the spilled salt, tossed it out the door, and crossed herself. Filling a kettle with water, she placed it on a burner and took two mugs out of a cabinet.

When Juliana left the kitchen and went into her room, Delia looked around. A few drops of her blood were drying on the floor tiles.

Juliana brought out a robe for Delia and fixed two steaming cups of sweetened tea. She offered one to Delia.

"Come outside with me, *niña*, there's still dew on the roses. The sun is about to rise." She put an arm around Delia and walked her out the door. "I am so glad to see Carnaval end."

❧

Delia Susana Pineda de Rubio opened her eyes.

Next to the bottles of perfume on her dresser, stood a silver frame with a photograph of *Doña* Berta Pineda flanked by her daughters María Elena and Delia, three captivating women wearing elegant *polleras*. On the back of the photograph Delia had written: "Martes de Carnaval, 1952."

A small cloth pouch, taped to the back of the frame, contained the braids that Papá had allowed her to cut off before her seventeenth birthday. "You are mature enough, *querida*," he had said, "You are the daughter of my heart."

She picked up the frame and looked at the photograph.

Mamá looked proud of her daughters and María Elena looked happy. That year she had returned from Argentina and married Rubén Madrigal. Nena called him her *gaucho*. They had met at the University in Buenos Aires. Rubén came from a wealthy cattle ranching family, whose land spread over a large expanse of the *pampas*. He adored Nena.

The Madrigals had traveled to Panamá for the wedding and Rubén's younger brother had been his best man. Delia and Josefita served as bridesmaids with four of María Elena's friends, and Isabel stood with María Elena as matron of honor. Toñito had been the ringbearer. Juliana had baked the wedding cake, her special *sopa borracha*.

Mamá beamed when Justo escorted her to the front pew and Papá was almost lost in the cloud of white satin and tulle in which María Elena floated as they marched down the aisle.

Pablo Luis Morán and his family had not been invited to María Elena's wedding.

Daniela Morán and Alberto Guzmán had a quiet wedding four months after that Ash Wednesday. A few months later a notice in the newspapers announced the birth of their son. The rumor was that he now kept a mistress in a *casa chica*.

Don Nacho recovered Mamá's medallion, but she never wore it again.

Delia felt a caress on her shoulder. She turned her head and kissed her husband's hand.

Juan Luis bent down and brushed the nape of her neck with his lips. He met her eyes, smiled at her and took the photograph from her hands. He looked at it for a moment.

"You look so much like your mother, *mi amor*. But there's a great difference, too."

Delia tilted her head, questioning.

"I don't see in your eyes the sadness that welled in *Doña* Berta's for so long."

He set the photograph on the dresser, took Delia's hands and helped her up.

Delia wrapped her arms around him, and kissed his neck. Then licked his lips slowly until he opened them. Her tongue darted around in his mouth and she imagined herself a hummingbird drinking nectar. Soon, she felt his arousal and took his hands.

"Come, *mi vida*, let's try to make a baby," Delia said, taking him to their bed.

"Already?" Juan Luis teased. "We've only been married two years!"

"But we waited four years as *novios*."

"You can blame *Don* Nacho for that. He wouldn't trust his daughter to a man without a formal career. A musician wasn't enough for him," he whispered, unbuttoning her dress.

"Yes, Doctor Rubio, Papá knew my worth."

She let the dress fall to the floor and playfully pushed him onto the bed, then straddled him.

"Now, be quiet and let me make love to you."

As she began to undress him, Juan Luis took Delia's right hand, the one with the faded burn scar on the back, and licked the scar that crossed the lines on her open palm, the one left by the knife she had given María Elena.

Delia caught her breath. Like that morning of Ash Wednesday, she soared, free.

She leaned toward his ear and whispered, her tongue darting to his earlobe now and then:

Dos rojas lenguas de fuego
que a un mismo tronco enlazadas,
se aproximan, y al besarse
forman una sola llama;
dos notas que del laúd
a un tiempo la mano arranca,
y en el espacio se encuentran
y armoniosas se abrazan . . .

Two red tongues of fire
intertwine on the same trunk,
come nearer,
and in kissing form a single flame;
two notes that from the lute
the hand at one time wrenches
meet in space
and embrace harmoniously . . .

"Your poem?"

"No, Gustavo Adolfo Bécquer. Justo calls him 'the Romantic Sevillano.' Do you like it?"

"I prefer the poetry in your caress," he said, changing position, allowing her to finish undressing him.

Delia looked at the only man she had ever desired, brushed back his hair, held his face in her hands, and leaned over to explore his mouth again. She continued touching, smelling, tasting every bit of him taking him through all her senses, until they changed position and his kiss sealed her lips.

Delia Pineda abandoned herself to her husband's embrace, ready to step into Paradise once more.